THE
DRAGON EGG
PRINCESS

ALSO BY ELLEN OH

Finding Junie Kim

A Thousand Beginnings and Endings

Spirit Hunters

Spirit Hunters #2: The Island of Monsters

Prophecy

Warrior

King

THE
DRAGON EGG
PRINCESS

ELLEN OH

HARPER

An Imprint of HarperCollinsPublishers

The Dragon Egg Princess
Text copyright © 2020 by Ellen Oh
Map artwork © 2020 by Sun Oh

Library of Congress Cataloging-in-Publication Data

Names: Oh, Ellen, author.
Title: The dragon egg princess / Ellen Oh.
Description: First edition. | New York, NY : Harper, an imprint of
    HarperCollinsPublishers, [2020] | Summary: "A magicless boy, a fierce
    bandit leader, and a lost princess must join forces to save their worlds from
    foreign forces and a long-forgotten evil that lurks in an ancient magical
    forest"— Provided by publisher.
Identifiers: LCCN 2019009514 | ISBN 9780062875808 (pbk.)
Subjects: | CYAC: Adventure and adventurers—Fiction. | Magic—Fiction. |
    Robbers and outlaws—Fiction. | Princesses—Fiction. | Good and evil—
    Fiction. | Fantasy.
Classification: LCC PZ7.O364 Dr 2020 | DDC [Fic]—dc23 LC record
    available at https://lccn.loc.gov/2019009514

Typography by Joel Tippie
21 22 23 24 25 PC/BRR 10 9 8 7 6 5 4 3 2 1
❖
First paperback edition, 2021

To all the kids who wish they could see a real dragon.

Me too.

CHAPTER 1

KOKO GAZED OUT into the garden, watching the delicate movements of a butterfly flutter by. The sun was setting in a dazzling display of pink and purple radiance, and her parents were tied up in tedious court proceedings. Koko just wanted to run outside and play with the garden gnomes. They came alive only at night and would be ripe for fivestone, their favorite game. Koko would never have guessed that gnomes, with their short arms and stubby hands, would be so good at tossing the stone and snatching up the other four so quickly.

The little princess grabbed her five colorful stones and put them in her pocket. This must have been the hundredth set of fivestones that she'd had to paint. Gnomes loved to steal them after the games were over, even when she won.

And they were notorious cheats; one would yank at her long blue-black locks or pinch her so hard that her golden skin would turn an angry red, while the other would make off with her fivestones. But still, they were a lot more fun than her lessons.

With a quick glance at her dozing tutor, Koko tiptoed out of the room and into the garden. She knew she wasn't supposed to stray from her tutor's side, but history was so boring, and it was so easy to cast a small sleeping spell.

Outside, she could see the gray outlines of the gnomes standing motionless under the rays of the setting sun. It wasn't dark enough for them to awaken. Koko sighed and dropped down onto the fragrant grass. She sat staring at the hole in the knee of her favorite black pants. With a twirling finger she chanted the sewing spell that she'd hear the maids use when they were working.

No needle no thread.
No needle no thread.
Bind together with magic instead.

The hole disappeared without any evidence it ever existed. Koko smiled proudly. She was a lot faster than any of the maids.

Something fluttered right by her nose, a vision of sparkling silvery light tinted with flecks of green. Koko blinked and rubbed her eyes. It was the most beautiful butterfly she'd ever seen. The wings looked like they were studded with diamonds and emeralds and laced with silver netting. She ran after it, trying to catch it gently with her hands. But the butterfly fluttered just slightly out of reach.

It flew in a slow but rambling course through the garden and out the palace gates. It took her past a pair of sleeping sentries and deep into the forest, where gradually the lights of the palace disappeared in the darkness of the woods. But Koko was unaware of her surroundings as she followed the brightly glowing butterfly away from her home.

A sudden loud snapping sound jolted Koko out of her spell, and she gazed around, uncertain as to her whereabouts. The darkness was oppressive, and the little girl felt fear clench at her chest as she looked all around her. Just then, the butterfly flew close and perched carefully on Koko's shoulder, as if it could sense her fright. Koko crowed with delight to see how close the beautiful creature was. As she raised her hand to capture it, the butterfly flew gently ahead, and Koko was captivated once again.

She followed the butterfly until it stopped in the middle of a clearing and perched on the large knot of a fallen tree covered in moss. The butterfly's beautiful wings fluttered ever so slowly. Koko sat next to the butterfly, staring at its delicate wings. Now she could see that they weren't jewel studded. Instead, small drops of dew seemed to be caught up all along the outline of its wings, which were shot through with silvery veins like cobwebs. It was still the most beautiful thing Koko had ever seen. She wanted to touch it. She wanted to hold it in her hands.

As she reached for the butterfly, something tapped on her leg.

Koko looked down and gasped. Hundreds of tiny green creatures surrounded her. For a moment, she thought they were plants, but as she looked closer, she saw they had alien faces and small leaf-shaped hands with which they were now poking her gently. Koko sat absolutely still, too scared to scream or move. The little creatures pressed closer, whispering in a strange little language that sounded like the rustling of leaves.

"Who are you? What do you want?" Koko asked, trying not to cry.

One small creature came closer, a tiny humming sound emanating from it, almost like the purr of a kitten. In its little leaf hand, it held a small orange-colored persimmon. It climbed onto Koko's lap and held out the tiny fruit. With a shaking hand, Koko accepted.

"Thank you," she said. Looking down at the fruit, she found it was a perfectly formed persimmon, except that it was no bigger than a grape.

The creature purred again. It pantomimed lifting its hand to its small mouth. Koko didn't want to offend it, but she'd been taught to be careful of the unknown. How did she know that the fruit wasn't poisonous? How did she know that these creatures weren't dangerous? The princess cautiously observed the tiny green folk surrounding her. Suddenly she knew with absolute certainty that they would never hurt her. She popped the fruit into her mouth and immediately, a sweet explosion of flavor overwhelmed her.

"Oh my goodness!" Koko smiled. "That was delicious! May I have some more, please?"

Excited, several of the creatures pressed more fruit into her hands, and Koko felt her fear dissipate as she sat and played with her new friends. Before long, she was chatting with them and learning their strange whispering language. She learned that they were called namushin, spirits of the Kidahara trees, and that they were so happy she was safely back home with them.

"But this is not my home," Koko replied in confusion. "I've never been here before."

The namushin rushed to tell her a wondrous story about a time long, long ago, when dragons soared the skies above them and magical creatures roamed the lands in peace.

Hours passed but Koko knew nothing of time. She never heard the frantic cries of her parents as they searched for her. She didn't hear the baying of the search dogs that circled the perimeter but could never quite find her. Secure in the company of her new friends, the princess followed the namushin into the hollow of an ancient tree and disappeared.

CHAPTER 2

Five years later . . .

"THE KING CANNOT be allowed to stand in the way of progress anymore! The railway must be built and connect us to our neighbors so that we can trade without fear of bandits and monsters. And the ban on mining in Kidahara Wilderness must be removed if the kingdom of Joson is to survive as a nation!"

Jiho Park sat and listened as the angry man with the northern accent and funny rounded hat yelled at the townspeople. It was market day, so the village was more crowded than usual. The angry man had driven into Hanoe village early that morning in an ornate horseless carriage from the north. The carriage had been enhanced by magic and included an entourage of red-uniformed soldiers who were not citizens of Joson. He said he was the voice of the people, but he called himself Lord Fairfax and dressed in ostentatious fashion, unusual for their kingdom. Tight jacket, tighter pants, and some silken thing that was elaborately tied around his neck. He stood out against the townspeople's loose jackets and trousers. The biggest tip-off was his sword. Swinging awkwardly against his hip, it was encrusted in jewels and fancier than any killing weapon had a right to be. Lord Fairfax was no soldier, that's for sure. He was just a glorified mouthpiece, and there was only one person in the entire kingdom he could be working for.

"If the king is not willing to do what is right for his people, then I fear the time may have come for him to step down and allow his brother, Prince Roku, to rule in his place."

Jiho snorted. Prince Roku was King Suri's younger half brother, the half being of Orion blood. He'd spent most of his childhood growing up in the kingdom north of Joson. His mother was a niece of the Orion king. Roku returned after her death five years ago to be an adviser in foreign affairs to King Suri. But everyone could see that what he really wanted was the throne.

"That's treason," someone muttered in the crowd. Even with the shocked murmurs, no one made a move against the loudmouthed lord. It was a sign of how bad the times were that such treason could be stated in public with no fear of any reprisals.

"But what of Princess Koko?" a hesitant voice asked. Jiho couldn't see who it was but guessed that it was the innkeeper's wife, who was a staunch royal supporter and still kept a portrait of the missing princess in her foyer. "If the train tracks are built and the Kidahara Wilderness mined, we may never see the princess again."

"Don't be stupid," Lord Fairfax sneered. "The princess is dead. She's been dead for five years. The king and queen have been living on a foolish hope that the creatures of the forest might one day return her."

He laughed derisively. "And this is exactly why we need a new, modern-thinking king like Prince Roku. Not one who still believes in the old stories, like the namushin."

Jiho smirked as he heard the angry response of the crowd. This close to the Kidahara, there was not one villager who didn't believe in the namushin, the tree spirits of the Kidahara. There were plenty of shrines to the namushin that dotted the entire Joson countryside. They were the most popular of all the magical creatures, because they were known to be peaceful and gentle and to help those who were lost in the Kidahara find their way out. The tree spirits were connected to all the trees of the Kidahara and knew all that was happening in their world. It was considered bad luck to talk ill of the namushin.

Not recognizing the mood of his audience, the loud-mouth continued to spout his propaganda.

"We must not allow sentiment to stop us from the future

potential of our country. Progress is the only way we will survive. The advanced technology of the other kingdoms, like Orion, puts our civilization to shame! The Botan bandits have increased their brazen thievery, and the Kidahara monsters have isolated us from the rest of the world. Now we must fight and take back what is rightfully ours!"

This time there was an answering murmur of agreement from some of the men, which was louder than the quieter pleas to support the royals. Jiho couldn't blame them. The last few years had been rough, and people were suffering. Food was scarce and work hard to come by. Something had to change.

"Starting tomorrow morning, our work crews will clear the Kidahara forest so that we can start to build the railway. We will work from Hanoe all the way to the border between Joson and Orion, where the railway companies are waiting to begin laying down the tracks. But they won't do it unless they can be assured that the tracks will lead somewhere. Specifically, here to Hanoe. Your village has been chosen to be the most important railroad station. A transport hub for all of Joson. Your economy will be revitalized and Hanoe will become the most influential village in all of Joson. More important than even the capital."

The first time the railway tried to put down tracks, they didn't even make it a day when the entire team of workers vanished without a trace. This time, the Orion men were starting from within the kingdom and working their way out. Jiho didn't see what difference it made; they would still have to go through Kidahara. And the forest didn't like humans.

"We need your help. We need local Hanoe men to go with our rail party and show them the way through the forest." Lord Loudmouth was finally getting to the heart of his speech. "You will be well compensated for your work. Ten pieces of silver per day."

The muttering of the crowd turned into surprise. Ten pieces of silver a day was a lot of money. Even Jiho found himself tempted by the offer. But not enough to venture into the Kidahara.

"Foolish men. They know not what they will unleash."

Jiho turned around to find the old lady monk, Yoon, squatting by his side.

"Where'd you come from?" he asked. He was always surprised at how stealthy the monk could be. "And what do you mean by that?"

Yoon straightened up and lowered her straw hat over her forehead, but not before Jiho caught the pitying look she gave him from her sharp green eyes. "Your father is one of the smartest rangers I know," the monk said. "He taught you to respect the forest."

A vision of his father filled Jiho's mind for a moment. He was a big, burly man with a shock of thick black hair that surrounded his serious face. It was a happier time when his father was still around, before his mother died.

Jiho looked away in bitter anger. "Don't talk about my father. He deserted us."

The monk shook her head and placed a gentle hand on his shoulder. "No, he didn't. The forest took him. For what reason, we don't know."

Furious, Jiho shook off her hand. "You're wrong. My father packed a bag and walked away. No explanation. The forest didn't take him. He abandoned us. Plain and simple."

"Nothing is ever that simple, my friend. Especially when it comes to this forest." She gestured to where the border of the Kidahara Wilderness ran past the eastern boundaries of the village.

Jiho shrugged. "Welcome to the story of my life."

"You are a Park," the monk replied. "You come from a long line of rangers. You know the dangers of the forest. The trees of the Kidahara are not like others. They are special. Your father knew which were safe and which would unleash the dark monsters. These men, with their fancy weapons and silly gadgets, know nothing."

Bitterness swelled within him. His father knew the Kidahara better than any person in the kingdom. And he had chosen it over his family. Jiho didn't want to hear about his father anymore.

"Perhaps it's time to burn down the forest and get rid of the monsters once and for all," he said. "After all, it's the Kidahara that keeps us from advanced technology. Even our closer neighbors have become modernized and can use small objects to talk over long distances."

"Modern witchcraft will never last! No, child, nothing

stops the forest," Yoon replied. "You know that. Don't listen to these men. We can't go against the Kidahara. It always wins."

Jiho hunched his shoulders. Picking up his knapsack of traded items, he started walking home.

"Dark times are coming, and the Kidahara knows," the monk yelled after him. "Remember, you're a ranger's son. When you are in the forest, you must think like your father."

Jiho snorted. He might be a ranger's son, but he hated the Kidahara. Jiho didn't want to learn about the forest and fighting off the more dangerous monsters. He never wanted to be a ranger. Jiho's talent was not in fighting or tracking, but in making things. Even though he was only fourteen years old, his stone arrowheads were top sellers at the marketplace. And it was his carving skills that kept his family from starving. Today, he'd traded his whole stock of arrowheads for a bag of rice and other badly needed supplies.

Jiho loved his uncle and aunt Lee and did everything he could to help around the farm. Not for fear of being kicked out. His uncle and aunt were the kindest and most loving people he knew. Not having any children themselves, they'd always doted on Jiho and his little sisters. Aunt Lee was his mother's older sister. When Jiho's mother died after giving birth to his youngest sister, it was Aunt Lee who came and took care of the baby. It was Uncle Lee who'd brought food and took care of them while Jiho's father wandered the forest alone. And five years ago, when Jiho's father packed a bag, along with his heavy walking stick, and walked out the door without a word, it was his uncle and aunt who'd come to pick them up and bring them to their new home.

This was not an easy thing for them to do, Jiho knew. Generations of Parks had lived for centuries on their homestead at the outskirts of the Kidahara. Their estate was long considered a magical void, because the Parks were the only people in Joson that nullified magic. Having Jiho and his sisters on the farm meant that the Lees couldn't use any of the magic spells to help them manage the work.

Which was why Jiho worked so hard. The past few years had been especially difficult on all the farms. But it hit theirs the hardest. His uncle's farm bordered too close to the Kidahara. With several seasons of poor harvests, their supplies were low. Jiho knew it was because of their presence that his uncle couldn't use growing spells or repelling spells. And in the house, his aunt couldn't even use a simple washing spell because of his sisters. He could feel how burdensome their presence was, and yet his uncle and aunt never complained.

To make up for the inconvenience of housing and caring for them, Jiho woke up early every morning to help his uncle around the farm and then carved his treasures into the wee hours of the night to make sure there would always be rice in his little sisters' bowls. But he worried that it wasn't enough.

As he walked out of town, he kept a wary eye on the

forest boundary. He hated the forest with a passion. It was still daylight, but one never knew what Kidahara creatures might be lurking in the shadows.

From ahead, he heard the steady approach of horse-less carriages. Stepping off the road to let them pass, Jiho stared curiously at the unusual vehicles. These were the larger horseless carriages called trucks, used in Orion, the closest neighboring kingdom. They were filled with men, women, and young boys, none of whom were from Joson. These machines usually couldn't survive this close to the forest. But like Lord Fairfax's fancy carriage, they'd all been enhanced by magic. Jiho whistled to himself. Someone had spent a fortune to magic them all.

Suddenly, the trucks came to an abrupt stop and Jiho became keenly aware of the change in the atmosphere of the Kidahara. Jiho had a sixth sense when it came to magical creatures. It was an ability all the members of his family had. He felt an intense chill and became aware of the unnatural silence. He could feel it in his stomach; the churning of his gut. Danger was near.

A few men on the trucks jumped off and started running into the forest. A man in a black suit stepped out of the lead truck and yelled in alarm. "Where are you guys going? Get back here this instant! That's an order!"

A sickly sweet aroma assaulted Jiho's nose, causing a wave of dizziness.

"Vorax," he whispered. He plugged his nose and breathed

through his mouth. Running toward the yelling man, he shouted, "Tell everyone to cover their noses and don't run into the forest!"

"But my men," the man in the black suit replied. Suddenly his angry expression turned strange and vacant. He swayed from side to side before trying to walk into the forest. Jiho grabbed him and pushed him back toward the truck.

"Let me go!" The man was trying to shove past Jiho. "I must find out who wears that glorious perfume. It smells like heaven."

"Boy, would you be surprised," Jiho said as he fought back the struggling man.

"Cover your noses!" he yelled at the Orion workers, staring from the trucks. "Tell everyone to cover their noses or they will run into the forest and be lost forever."

Two men with face masks came and grabbed the man in the suit and pulled him back into the truck, while another group of masked soldiers approached Jiho. They wore dark green uniforms and carried what looked sort of like a rifle, but with strange attachments like nothing Jiho had seen before. Before Jiho could figure out what they were, the lead soldier motioned him forward.

"Boss man says we need all our crew," the lead soldier said. "Do you know where they went?"

Jiho sighed. The last thing he wanted to do was enter the Kidahara, but he knew exactly what had happened to the

Orion men, and he couldn't in good conscience leave them to their fate. It was too horrible.

He dropped his knapsack on the side of the road.

"Follow me," he said. "But be quiet. We don't want to invite anything else to this party."

He took in whiffs of the sickly aroma to locate where the Vorax could be. The Vorax's magic didn't work on Jiho, but the smell made him nauseous.

"What was that odor?" the leader asked. "Why aren't you covering your nose?"

"Magic doesn't work on me," Jiho explained. "I'm immune to it."

"Magic?" the leader asked incredulously. "You're saying magic caused our workers to run into the forest?"

"It's a Vorax," Jiho said. "A spiderlike creature that lures its prey with an aroma that bewitches humans into its web and then eats them."

"A spider? Just how big is it?"

"It's bigger than your truck," Jiho said.

At his words, the Orion men grew silent.

Jiho moved swiftly through the forest, easily following the trail of the four men. The sickly odor was so strong he could taste it.

He put up a finger to his mouth to warn the others. "We're close, please be very quiet."

Slowly creeping forward, he led the soldiers around a

clump of trees and froze. A gigantic web sprawled through a large open space and was woven around the trunks of nearly ten trees that surrounded it. Trapped along one section of the web were the unmoving forms of four Orion workers. But the worst part of it all was the enormous black Vorax in the center, busily wrapping one of the men into a silken cocoon, using six of its twelve long hairy legs.

"That's the biggest web I've ever s—" The voice trailed off as the soldiers took in the horror of the Vorax for the first time.

The legs of the Vorax stopped, and it began to turn its body around as Jiho and the men frantically ducked out of sight. If the back of a Vorax was frightening, the front was far worse. Twelve large red eyes and a gaping mouth, with pincers dripping acid that burned through the foliage below it.

"So if magic doesn't work on you, then that thing can't hurt you, right?" the lead soldier whispered.

Jiho glared in annoyance. "That thing doesn't need magic to kill me."

"I say we shoot it," another soldier offered.

Jiho shook his head. "It has an impenetrable shell. All you'll do is make it mad."

"So what do we do?"

"I'm going to make a birdcall," Jiho said.

"A what?"

Ignoring the soldiers, Jiho remembered the training that

he had done with his father the first time they'd trekked through the Kidahara. He could hear his father's voice in his head.

The only thing that a Vorax fears is the Aquila. Even the mere hint of its call will send the Vorax scuttling away to its deepest den.

The Aquila was one magical being that Jiho had never seen in the Kidahara. He knew of it only from books and hand drawings that were in his father's library. It was the largest bird in the world. An eagle with the body of a lion. With a resolute nod, Jiho turned to the Orions.

"As soon as you see the Vorax enter its burrow, you have to cut the men down as quickly as possible," Jiho said. "But be careful not to tug at the strings, just slice them with your knife, or the Vorax will be having a smorgasbord for dinner tonight."

The soldiers pulled out their knives and stood behind Jiho, who moved as close to the web as he dared. Cupping his mouth, he let out a loud piercing caw with a deep shrill. The Vorax froze. But as soon as Jiho let out another round of caws, it skittered backward into a large burrow at the other end of the web.

"Now," Jiho said.

They all rushed under the web to free the trapped men. Jiho crawled to the farthest man, the one who was being cocooned, and sliced the silky threads free until the man fell to the ground. Jiho cut the dazed man out of the cocoon and gave him a hard slap.

"We have to get out of here," Jiho whispered, and urged the man to begin crawling out from under the web. But as they reached the others, Jiho noticed the web begin to tremble. He looked up to see that while all the trapped men had been freed, one of the Orion rescuers had gotten her arm entangled in the web.

"Stop moving!" he whispered as loud as he could, but it was too late. They heard a chittering sound and watched in horror as the Vorax emerged from its burrow once more.

Jiho tried his Aquila call again, but this time the Vorax would not be fooled.

"Run!" he screamed as he cut through the threads holding the trapped soldier and pushed her free.

They all fled for their lives, just in time. Jiho glanced behind him to see the Vorax bound off the web and into the trees above them, nearly bending them horizontal with its weight. Then, with another mighty jump, the Vorax leaped in front of them and let out a high-pitched shriek. It stopped the team in their tracks, screaming from the pain in their eardrums. Jiho, unbothered by the magical shriek, whipped out his slingshot, picked up several large stones, and aimed them right into the Vorax's cavernous jaws. As the enormous spider gagged, Jiho led the agonized Orions away.

The reprieve lasted seconds before the Vorax bounded into the trees again. Its twelve eyes were now fixated on

Jiho, and it jumped into the tree directly in front of him.

Jiho screeched to a halt and tried to backpedal as he watched the Vorax readying itself for the attack. But then a thunderous caw filled his ears. The skies darkened as a mighty wind assailed them. Before the Vorax could move, gigantic lion's claws pierced through its mighty shell, sending twelve of the spider's legs flailing in pain. A large eagle's beak caught hold of a few legs and ripped them off, swallowing them in a quick gulp. The eagle's head turned its golden eye on Jiho and once again let out its booming caw. It nodded as if to say thank you for the meal and then spread its wings and soared into the sky, carrying the Vorax in its claws.

Jiho collapsed onto the ground.

He had finally seen the mysterious Aquila.

CHAPTER 3

JIHO LED THE stunned group of Orions back to where their trucks had stopped. The boss man, whom Jiho had pushed to safety, was yelling at a whole bunch of people just as he spotted them returning. He broke into a relieved smile and hurried over.

"Palmers, you got everyone back safely!"

The man he called Palmers wiped a shaky hand across his forehead. "If it wasn't for this kid, we would've all been dead."

The rescued men were finally beginning to recover from their shock. But one was still blubbering and raging about the gigantic spider. He ran over to the boss man and shook him hard.

"Boss, I can't do it! I have to go home! I'm not going into

that hellhole again! They'll kill us! They'll kill us all!"

The boss gestured for the soldiers to take the screaming man away and turned to shake Jiho's hand.

"Thanks a million, kid! You just saved me a whole lot of headaches and paperwork," he said. Reaching into his pocket, he pulled out a small bag that clinked in a musical jangle. "Here's a little reward for your troubles."

Jiho accepted the bag with a bow. He picked up his things and was turning to leave when the boss called out to him again.

"Hey, what's your name, kid?"

"Jiho Park."

"Listen, Jiho, we could really use someone like you who knows this place. Why don't you join us? We pay ten silver pieces a day and three square meals. But for you, I'd give you twenty a day."

"Twenty? Why so much for me?" Jiho asked.

"Because you know these woods and we don't," the boss man said, in all seriousness. "I mean, we got some locals on staff here, but they had no idea what was even going on! I need you. And I promise to make it worth your while."

Once again Jiho was tempted. He'd made only ten silver pieces for two weeks' worth of carving.

"I'm sorry, but my family needs me," he said. But he paused, curious about something.

"Excuse me, how is it that you and all your workers can speak Joson so well?" Jiho asked.

The man pointed at a small silver disc attached to his belt. "It's the universal translator," he said with a smile. "It translates Joson, Bellprix, Urcian, you name it, it translates it into good old Orion."

"But you are speaking Joson now," Jiho said in confusion.

"Yeah, whatever special enhancements you people put on our universal translators are the most amazing thing! It translates any language into your native language, so that you hear it immediately. Brilliant, isn't it? If you work for me, you can have one of your very own."

Unless the universal translator could translate for the magical creatures in the Kidahara, Jiho didn't think it was that useful.

"Sorry, I've got to go now," he said.

"If you change your mind, come find me in town, the name's Murtagh. Brock Murtagh," the man shouted after him.

Jiho shook his head as he continued walking. What was it with people shouting things at him today? He sighed at the idea of all that money. The only thing that really kept him from taking the job was the idea of going back into the Kidahara. Seeing a Vorax and an Aquila in the same day was more than enough for a lifetime. Well, at least he got a reward for saving the men. He looked into the bag of coins the boss had given him and froze in shock. It looked like at least five gold coins.

A fortune.

The exhaustion and trauma of the near-death experience faded as exhilaration filled Jiho. He couldn't wait to give it to his uncle and aunt. Here was finally hope for surviving the coming winter. With a wide grin showcasing his deep dimples, Jiho sprinted the rest of the way back to his uncle's farm, only to freeze in horror.

The small farmstead he'd left behind in the morning was completely destroyed.

CHAPTER 4

HIS AUNT CALLED out his name in relief and pulled him into a tight embrace. His little sisters, Hana and Sera, huddled close to their aunt. Everyone was crying.

"It was a tornado!" Sera, the youngest, cried out. "If Auntie hadn't seen it coming, it would have swept us all away!"

Hana wiped her eyes, trying to calm down. At nine, she was very serious and responsible. "Uncle got us all down into the root cellar. But we didn't have time to save any of the animals."

She began to weep again, and Jiho hugged her tight. Hana had always been close to the farm animals, feeding them every day.

"We're glad you weren't here," his aunt whispered. "What

if you'd been taken by the tornado?"

"What do you mean taken?" Jiho asked.

"There was something strange and unnatural about it," his aunt explained. "Look how it hit only our land and none of the surrounding areas."

Jiho was struck by the truth of her words. A tornado should have devastated the entire area, but the surrounding woods were completely untouched.

"Where's Uncle?" Jiho asked.

The girls pointed into the field. They could see a dejected figure standing in the middle of the empty space. Jiho walked over with a heavy heart. There was nothing left. The entire farm had been ripped apart. And the cows, pigs, and chickens they depended upon were dead or gone.

His uncle turned at his approach. His usual serious expression had turned pale and grim.

"I'm going to have to send your aunt and the girls to my sister's place in Iri village," he said. "But their house is too small to take either of us in. We'll have to look for work and camp out for a while."

"What are you thinking of doing?" Jiho asked.

"There's work at the iron mill over in Naga," his uncle replied. "Might even let us sleep in the factory if we're lucky."

Jiho's heart sank. The iron mill was a death trap. More men and women died every day in the factories than from bandits or monsters. And at three pieces of silver a day, the pay wasn't worth the risk. The only place worse was the mines. But the mine owners didn't use human workers.

"Uncle, you can't work there. It'll kill you."

Uncle shook his head. "There's not much choice, son. We've lost everything. We need money to rebuild."

"I was in town today and some Orion men were there. They wanted me to work for them in clearing the forest. They offered me twenty silver a day. I can go join them."

His uncle immediately shook his head. "No way we're going to work with any Orions. They are untrustworthy backstabbers. Just look at Prince Roku."

It troubled Jiho that his beloved uncle could be so close-minded. While it was true that Roku was not a good man, Jiho did not believe that all Orions were bad. "But it's twenty silver per day! That's a fortune! We would never make anywhere near that at the mill!"

His uncle's face was grim and unmoving.

"We're safer at the mill than in Kidahara. You know how dangerous the forest is. No, let's not take any chances."

Jiho's lips tightened mulishly. "Uncle, you can't go to the mill. You'll catch iron lung. It would destroy my aunt and the girls. You have to stay here and start rebuilding. I'll get the money you need."

His uncle looked uneasy. "It's not just the Orions that's the problem. I don't want you messing with the Kidahara. Remember what your father always said—"

"My father isn't here," Jiho said sharply. He opened his

bag and took out all the supplies, the money he got from selling his arrowheads, and the bag of gold coins.

"Uncle, the reason I'm so late is because I helped save some Orion men who wandered into the Kidahara. They paid me in gold coins." Jiho handed everything to his uncle. "That means you don't have to go anywhere. You just need to start rebuilding so that my aunt and sisters can have a home again. I'll make more money and help rebuild the farm with you. If I go now, I can catch up with the men before sunset."

His uncle grabbed his shoulders in alarm. "Your father went into the Kidahara, and we've never seen him again. Jiho, you're more than a nephew, you're like my son. I don't want to lose you too!"

Jiho smiled. "I'll be careful. I still remember all the things my father taught me about the forest. I'll be fine."

His uncle argued on, pleading with him not to go. But Jiho refused to change his mind.

With a frustrated groan, his uncle gave in.

"You are so stubborn, just like your father," he complained. He hugged Jiho hard. "Be smart, and be safe. Promise you'll come home to us."

Jiho bowed. "Nothing can keep me away."

He looked toward the wreckage of the farmhouse and watched his aunt and sisters picking through the rubble. He stared hard, committing them to his memory. This was all that was left of his family.

"I'm going to go without saying goodbye to them," he said. "They won't understand; they'll try to stop me."

His uncle nodded, his eyes sorrowful as he gazed back at his nephew. "I'll take care of it. Don't worry."

Jiho studied his uncle's concerned face and felt a rush of affection and deep gratitude. His uncle and aunt provided Jiho and his sisters with love and a home when they needed it the most. Jiho would do anything to help them now in their hour of need.

Jiho bowed and then hugged his uncle. "Thanks, Uncle. I'll come home soon. I promise."

With one last look at his family, Jiho turned and ran for the road.

CHAPTER 5

WHEN JIHO WAS little, his father would take him into the forest. His father taught him how to choose a tree and pray to its spirit before chopping it down. At those times, Jiho would always shudder. It felt as if an unseen being had walked through him. But he never felt that he was in danger. It wasn't just that he felt safe being with his father. It was the knowledge that the forest would not hurt them.

Some days they would walk through the forest for hours, searching for the elusive gateway to the magic realm, called Nackwon. His father was sure he would find it one day, but Jiho wasn't sure he wanted to. It was the kingdom of the fairies, witches, and all the magical creatures, and it was far more dangerous than the Kidahara.

Jiho's father used to share the old legends with Jiho every

night before bedtime. His favorite story was of the day magic entered their world. He remembered hearing it for the first time when he was five years old.

"A long time ago, our world had no magic," his father said. "In fact, it was quite boring."

"You mean, like the other kingdoms are now?"

"Yes, just like them! The forest was just a forest. A tree was just a tree. And then one day, dragons suddenly appeared in the skies above the Kidahara. They were the first magical creatures that humans had ever seen. Frightened, the people reacted badly, as they often do when faced with something they don't understand. It was the humans who attacked the dragons first. Killed them. And it caused trouble between our worlds."

"What was the other world, Papa?"

"The Nackwon. The magic realm that exists in the Kidahara. No human has ever seen it."

"Then how do we know it is real?"

His father laughed. "Some things don't need to be seen to be believed. You know it's real because your heart tells you it is. Anyway, the Nackwon became very afraid of humans. So their leader, Empress Luzee, waged a terrible war against the humans. The Great War between our worlds lasted for years as magical creatures invaded our lands and killed many people. And then one day all the dragons disappeared, and the creatures of the Nackwon retreated back into the Kidahara."

"What happened to the dragons?"

"I heard that they all died. But that always made me sad."

"I wish I could see a dragon, Papa!"

"Me too, Jiho."

Walking along the road bordering the Kidahara, Jiho was flooded with memories of his father. Hunting for wild game, foraging for edible roots and mushrooms, leaving offerings for the namushin. There were so many memories of joyful times deep in the Kidahara with his father.

But now it felt too dangerous and mysterious. His father had been his safety net. Jiho didn't have the same comfort that he used to. He avoided the Kidahara like the plague. So what was he doing thinking of joining a foreign crew to help clear the forest? His father would have yelled at him. Told him he was crazy to help anyone who would harm his beloved forest. Jiho wondered if his father had ever found his way to the Nackwon. Maybe his father was stuck there, trapped by the fairies and unable to return home. That's what happened in fairy tales. Magical creatures loved to trap or kidnap humans and keep them for their entertainment. Then after a few days, when the human was finally set free, he'd wander home only to find that it hadn't been just a few days but a hundred years. The problem with that story was that his father had been the one to voluntarily leave in the first place.

Anger flooded him again at the thought. All his father

ever worried or cared about was the forest. What good was it to him? Why should he care if it was all razed to the ground? His father had tried to convince him for years that it was his destiny to be a ranger, just like all Parks before him. But Jiho was not interested. He didn't want to be a ranger. He didn't even want to be a Park anymore.

Just then, something moved in the brush near the forest side of the road. Fear and his wild imagination sent Jiho careening down the road back to town. He didn't want to be this close to the forest when darkness hit. It just wasn't safe.

Oh, and joining the Orion crew to systematically chop down the Kidahara trees is safer? a small voice inside him asked. Jiho shook his head, refusing to think beyond the twenty silver pieces per day he'd been offered. Besides, at least he wouldn't be alone in the forest.

It was completely dark by the time Jiho made it back to Hanoe village. But it wasn't hard to see where the Orion company were. Their trucks took up the entire town center, and Orion employees and soldiers were camped out in every corner of the open area.

As Jiho approached, a soldier stepped forward to block his path.

"What's your business here?" the soldier asked.

"I'm here to see Mr. Murtagh about a job," Jiho responded.

The soldier peered closer at Jiho's face. "Hey, weren't you the kid who helped get our men back from the Kidahara?"

Jiho nodded, relieved when the soldier started smiling.

"Those were some cool moves you had back there." The soldier shook his hand. "Boss was sorry to see you go. He'll be real happy you came back. I'll take you to his tent."

The soldier took Jiho to a large tent where a ruddy-faced middle-aged man with a smoking device chomped between his yellowed teeth sat tapping into a small thin glass and metal box while sitting at a messy desk. At the soldier's explanation, the man waved dismissively, and the soldier left.

The man began to speak to Jiho, but it was in the Orion language. Heaving an exasperated sigh, the man searched through the pile of papers on his desk until he found his universal translator. He switched it on and clipped it to his shirt.

"I'm Stu Nelson, the foreman. I'll take you to Mr. Murtagh as soon as I finish this report," he said brusquely.

Jiho looked around the large tent as the foreman tapped into his device and blew a stream of disgusting smoke. It made Jiho gag and his eyes water. He was just about to step out of the tent when he saw a large map on the table next to the foreman. It was a map of Joson with the Kidahara Wilderness highlighted in red. There were a lot of things pinned on it that Jiho didn't understand. But next to it, there were other papers that looked like future plans for the razed areas. They included buildings and factories to be located right within the heart of the wilderness. It appeared that the Orion men were planning more than building a railroad and mining. They were going to raze the entire Kidahara and build industrialized cities.

Jiho was both awed and troubled by the scope of the project. The Kidahara Wilderness was so big that it took up more than half the kingdom. It's why their people had been suffering. Lack of land and a growing population meant overcrowding and scarcity of resources. The expansion of the kingdom into the wilderness could save lives. It could revitalize their country. This had to be all good, right?

Yet a part of him worried what would happen to their country without the forest. And what would happen to the Nackwon? Legend stated that the Nackwon existed in the deepest parts of the Kidahara, where no man was allowed to trespass unless by invitation of a magical being. If the Kidahara was razed, would the Nackwon be exposed? Would it cause another war of the worlds?

"So what do you think of our master plan?" the foreman asked.

"Very ambitious," Jiho answered cautiously.

The foreman nodded. "Yes sirree, we've got some big plans for this area. It's gonna be the future of this kingdom! Bring it out of ancient times and into the modern age. And in the process, make a whole lot of money for us!"

He tapped at the logo prominently displayed on the board. It was a picture of a tree with foreign words written across the trunk of the tree.

"What's this?" Jiho asked.

"That's the Omni Murtagh Inc. logo," the foreman said.

"Omni Murtagh?" Jiho asked. They were strange sounding words to him.

"That's my company's name. You know Murtagh, like the boss you met today. Well technically, his father's company. He's out here trying to prove to his daddy that he is a worthy heir." The foreman snorted and shook his head.

Jiho thought there was a foreboding quality to the name of the company. It felt heavy, uneasy. He couldn't help but wonder what he'd gotten himself into as he followed the foreman out of the tent to find Mr. Murtagh.

The foreman walked Jiho over to the local tavern. Inside, he led him to a back table where a group of men were playing cards with the tavern owner, Mr. Mori.

"Where's the boss?" the foreman asked.

One of the men pointed toward the back, where Jiho spotted Murtagh talking with a woman in a hooded cape. There was something strange about the woman. Her gray hooded cloak hid most of her features, except for her long white hair and slender pale hands. Something about her gave Jiho an odd feeling, deep in his gut. It was similar to the feeling he would get when faced with a magical being. But what would such an entity be doing out of the Kidahara? And why would she be talking to an Orion, of all people? It made no sense. He was probably wrong, but he wondered who she could be.

Jiho stepped forward to take a closer look, but she slipped into darkness and disappeared.

As soon as Murtagh spotted Jiho, he broke into a toothy grin and threw open his arms as he walked over.

"Well, hey, I think my luck just changed," he said as he shook Jiho's hand. "I was hoping you'd change your mind, son."

He turned to the other men. "Do you know this kid? He saved my men from being eaten by a gigantic spider today."

Mr. Mori nodded. "Jiho's a good boy, but don't let him get too close to your magicked trucks or they'll stop working."

"What's that?" Murtagh turned to Jiho with a slight frown. "Our trucks cost us a small fortune to get them running smoothly through Joson. Without the magic enhancements, the trucks are useless here."

"Jiho is a Park, and Parks have no magic," Mr. Mori said. "In fact, magic doesn't work around them at all."

Murtagh frowned as he stared at Jiho in concern.

"And that's why I was able to save your men today," Jiho said. "The Vorax's magic didn't affect me like it did you."

Murtagh's face changed as he remembered the day's events. "That's right, it was that smell. It was so powerful that I felt I had to go to it—but you stopped me. That's how you were able to save my men."

Murtagh started smiling again. "Shoot, I think this really is my lucky day! You'll be our good luck charm to get safely through the Kidahara! Just be sure you don't take down my trucks!"

Jiho raised a reassuring hand. "It's okay, I'll make sure to stay far away from them. I'll just have to figure out another way to travel with you guys."

"I've got that covered," Murtagh said. "You think you can ride a motorbike?"

Jiho was confused. "What's a motorbike?"

Murtagh laughed. "You'll be fine, kid. I'm gonna get you into the Kidahara with us even if I have to get you a mule!" He turned to the foreman, who'd been secretly trying to sneak a drink from the bottle at the table. "Stu, take him to the scouts."

The foreman was surly as he led Jiho through the encampment again, refusing to answer any questions. Jiho was starting to wonder if the foreman's universal translator was not working when they arrived at a small campsite filled with young teens sitting around a fire.

"These kids here are like the Global United Nations. They represent all of the world—Orion, Urcia, Cloverly, Bellprix, and now Joson," he said, waving at Jiho.

"Okay, kiddos, this here is Jiho, and he's gonna be our local boy who helps lead the way. So give him a good old Omni Murtagh welcome and teach him the ropes." With a nod at Jiho, the foreman stomped off, leaving a trail of smoke behind.

Two older boys came over to greet him. They both had

medium brown skin and thin but muscular frames. The tallest and strongest-looking of the boys smiled at him.

"Hey, my name is Calvin Watson," he said, holding his hand out. His eyes were sharp but friendly.

It took Jiho a moment to remember that people outside of Joson liked to shake hands in greeting. Quickly he shook hands, wincing at the tight grip of Calvin's hand. The other boy reached over to shake his hand also.

"I'm Shane Gilman," he said. "Me and Calvin are from Bellprix. Boy, am I glad to see you! These woods give me the creeps. I sure would like to know what we gotta watch out for in there."

Jiho didn't understand why the woods made Shane want to crawl around on the floor, but he understood the rest of the question.

"The Kidahara is very ancient and powerful," Jiho said. "Many dangerous creatures make their home in the forest."

"Just how dangerous?" Shane asked. "What kinds of creatures are we talking about? Vampires? Werewolves?"

Jiho was confused. He didn't recognize any of these words. "Pardon? I don't know what that means."

"You know—vampires? Bloodsuckers? Werewolves? Half human, half wolf, rip your face off and eat it for a midnight snack?"

"Ah, interesting," Jiho said. "We have different creatures. Some eat humans, and some like to kidnap them. But most have magical powers."

"Magic? There's no such thing as magic, Jiho," Shane said. "Monsters are just monsters. Ain't nothing special about them."

This made Jiho pause. If his new friends didn't believe in magic, he feared that they would not make it through the Kidahara.

"Magic is what makes your trucks move around here," he said.

The boys laughed. "Jiho, those trucks have engines and run on petrol. There's nothing magical about that," Calvin said.

Jiho scratched his head. It seemed they knew nothing about the country that they had come to work in.

"I must explain something very important to you," he said. "Magic is real. You will see for yourself when we enter the Kidahara tomorrow. The forest does not like your modern mechanics and technology. For years, people outside of Joson could not navigate through our country unless they were on horseback. Your vehicles would die within coming a few feet of the Kidahara. That is why your company paid a lot of money for magic spells to make them work. Do you notice anything different about your vehicles?"

The boys looked at each other. "You're talking about the special enhancements on all the machinery, right? I wondered why there's no exhaust coming out of any of the trucks," Calvin said slowly. "And we never stopped at any refilling stations."

Jiho nodded. "I don't even know what exhaust or a refilling station is. We don't have trucks or cars or motorbikes here. Anything that does work here has been magicked. Do you not know the history of Joson?"

His new friends shook their heads. "We don't learn a lot about Joson," Calvin said. "Only that you guys are very behind in your technology."

"Behind? They don't have any!" Shane snorted.

"Joson is a very ancient country, and the Kidahara makes up most of our kingdom," Jiho said. "It is huge and has never been completely explored. That's because it is dangerous territory. There are many supernatural forces at work in the Kidahara. You must respect the magic, or you won't make it out of there alive."

Shane's smiling face changed while Calvin, who'd been quietly listening, stood very still.

"I think I want to hear all about the Kidahara tonight," Calvin said. "But let's get some dinner first."

He put a companionable arm around Jiho's shoulders and steered him to a large truck that looked like a moving café.

"What do you want to eat?" Calvin asked. "They've pretty much got the staples of all the cuisines here. Orion hot dogs, Urcian creamy noodles, Cloverly fish and chips, Bellprix spicy seafood stew—you name it and they can probably make it taste absolutely . . . terrible."

Jiho laughed. "What's the least terrible?"

Calvin and Shane looked at each other. Shane shook his head.

"Dude, these guys have such a special talent that even toast tastes bad," Shane said.

"It's okay, I'm pretty hungry," Jiho said.

"Hmmmm, you like pizza?" Shane asked.

"Never had it," Jiho replied.

"Good, then you won't know how disappointing it actually is." Calvin smiled and ordered the meal from the surly-looking server at the counter.

Jiho quickly ate the greasy cardboard-like food and washed it down with a chocolate drink that was far more enjoyable.

"Well, the chocolate drink was good," he said.

"That's cause the drinks are all bottled, and they can't mess it up with their nasty cooking," Shane replied.

"Hey! I can hear you!" the surly server replied.

"The truth will set you free!" Shane yelled back.

Calvin laughed. "Come on, Jiho, let's introduce you to the gang."

He walked toward another group of young teenagers sitting around a campfire.

"I hate this place," a pale boy with light blond hair and strange-colored eyes was saying. "No electricity. No computers. It's like the land that time forgot."

Calvin stepped forward. "That's why we're here. To bring the modern world to Joson." He pushed Jiho in front of him. "Speaking of Joson, this here is Jiho, and he's gonna teach us about this forest."

The pale boy jumped to his feet and pumped Jiho's hand enthusiastically. Jiho could now see that the boy had eyes as blue as the morning sky. "I'm Frankie. I come from Brookland, Orion," he said. "I'm glad to meet you. Not too many of you guys have joined us. There's only three that I know of, and they're all with the tree-cutting crews. I mean, we're the scouts. We have to clear the areas before anyone else. Shouldn't we have a local person first? How do we know where we're going without someone to guide us? Let me tell you, I wasn't looking forward to going in there without a local. I heard too many strange stories, you know what I'm saying?"

Jiho knew exactly what he was saying. But before he could respond, Frankie was introducing him to the rest of the group.

"That's Buddy. He's from Orion like me. Mac and Gabriel are from Cloverly. They hardly ever speak except to play their stupid Quest game. And that's Tess and Jay, and they hardly ever shut up," he said as he pointed to each of the team members.

Buddy, Mac, and Gabriel waved and quickly turned back to huddle together over what looked like cards with moving holograms. Jiho barely got a glance at them. But the two girls named Tess and Jay stood up and unleashed a torrent of abuse so fast and so loud Jiho couldn't understand any of it. The translator just gave up and let out beeping sounds. They were both quite tall and vibrantly attractive. Tess was a curvy girl with very curly golden brown hair that matched her golden brown skin perfectly. Jay had auburn hair and warm beige skin.

"Tess and Jay are from Urcia," Frankie said. "Whatever enhancements you people made to the universal translators has made it much easier and faster to understand them. Now we don't have to hear the long translation before we finally figure out what they're saying."

"That's 'cause Urcian is the most long-winded language in the world," Shane cut in.

"Just because we like to take our time and use our words wisely, you mock us," the girl named Tess drawled. "You are all brutes who do not understand the power of language."

"Shut up," Frankie said companionably.

The two Urcian girls launched into a long and eloquent tirade about what Frankie should do to himself. The others burst into laughter, but Jiho was perplexed.

Jiho scratched his head. "So I'm speaking Joson, and to me it sounds like you are speaking Joson too. But what language do you hear me speak?"

"You're speaking good old Orion, without any accent either," Frankie said. "And to them, we're all speaking Urcian."

"But not as poetically or as beautifully as a true Urcian," Jay retorted.

As Frankie and the Urcians continued to trade insults, Jiho sat down in front of the fire next to Shane.

"So the universal translator usually doesn't work like this?" Jiho asked.

"Nope, it was kind of slow, because it had to first translate the words into the language of the person wearing it."

"But what caused it to do this?"

Shane was shaking his head. "I don't know, buddy. You tell me."

"I'm not Buddy. That person over there is Buddy. I am Jiho."

Shane started laughing. "That's one thing the translator was never good at." He was shaking his head. "Buddy is his name, but it's also something we call someone we're friendly with."

"I understand," Jiho said. "But why are you asking me to tell you about the translators? I don't know anything about them."

Calvin interjected in his calm, thoughtful manner. "Maybe it's the magic you've been talking about. We've been calling them enhancements without really knowing what it is." He pointed back toward the foreman's tent. "Maybe it's messing with our equipment."

This was intriguing. "I know the forest does not like technology—it usually kills it," Jiho said thoughtfully. "But I never thought its magic could enhance man-made technology."

"Didn't you get one of your own?" Calvin asked. He held out his translator to Jiho.

Jiho shook his head. "I don't need it," he said, not explaining about his magic-canceling abilities. Staring at the small translator, he said, "So when it comes down to it, the Kidahara is stronger than technology."

Everyone turned to stare at Jiho in disbelief before bursting out in laughter.

"No way," Frankie said. "See that truck over there?"

He pointed at a large truck guarded by several soldiers who were holding strange black objects.

"There's enough firepower in it to blow up the entire forest to smithereens," he said. "Ain't no magic gonna withstand that!"

Firepower? Smitherwhat? Jiho didn't understand what they were talking about.

"I don't think the new guy's ever seen an assault rifle before," Frankie said. He stood up and went over to a nearby guard and came back with a long black object.

Calvin immediately stood up with a serious expression. "Frankie, you shouldn't be messing with that thing."

"We're not supposed to even touch one of those!" Shane exclaimed.

"Relax! I just want to show Jiho what a real rifle looks like," Frankie retorted.

"That's a rifle?" Jiho asked. "It doesn't look anything like the ones we have."

"Your rifles are ancient. These are the most modern weapons you can find," Frankie said, admiring it with lustful eyes.

"Shut up, Frankie." Tess stood up to face the Orion boy. "They are dangerous weapons, not something to be admired." She tried to take the rifle away, but Frankie sidestepped her.

"Hands off, Tess," Frankie said testily. "I'm just gonna show the new guy what it looks like."

"I know it's hard, Frankie, but try not to do anything stupid," Jay said with a long-suffering sigh.

"Oh, would you guys just lighten up already!" Frankie retorted.

He plopped down next to Jiho and cradled the weapon lovingly in his arms.

"This here is the Warrior 5000X series semiautomatic," he said. He then launched into a long description that was baffling to Jiho except for the last part, where he said, "It can blow a hole the size of a grapefruit in a tree."

Frankie handed it to Jiho. "Feel the power."

Jiho looked it over doubtfully. "I'm not sure it will work any better on magical creatures than our rifles," he said. Pointing it up as he passed it back, his hand slipped down and depressed some kind of a lever. Suddenly, the rifle let out a rapid-fire *ratatat* noise so loud it left a painful ringing in Jiho's ears. Frankie shrieked and snatched the rifle away. Leaves rained down on them, and several small birds fell dead to the ground.

Soldiers came running toward them, their weapons drawn as Calvin began yelling at Frankie.

"Why didn't you make sure the safety was on?"

"I don't know! I thought it was on!"

"I told you not to be stupid!" Jay yelled.

Even the three Quest-playing boys muttered angry curse words as they went to pick up their scattered cards.

The soldier who'd lent the rifle to Frankie grabbed it back and gave Frankie a hard slap on the back of his head. As they realized there was no danger, the other soldiers left.

But Jiho sat staring in stunned dismay at the dead birds on the ground.

"That is a terrible weapon," he said finally. "It means instant death to anything you point it at."

"Yeah, pretty much," Shane said. "Now you see why we're not afraid of your forest."

Troubled by his words, Jiho studied the camp again, noticing how many soldiers carried rifles. There must have been hundreds of them.

Threats. The forest would see them all as threats and would eat them alive. The weapons would bring more violence and more death.

Jiho shuddered. He didn't know where that thought came from, but he felt uneasy.

"What's the matter, Jiho?" Calvin asked. The older boy

was staring intently at him.

Jiho blinked and focused on the boys sitting all around the fire. "Don't underestimate the Kidahara forest," he said. The others quieted down at his words. "It is the most ancient land in our entire world. Old as time itself. And it is very dangerous."

All the others scoffed at him except for Calvin and Shane.

"Jiho, I'm sorry to say this, but your backward country is not going to be able to hold up against the Omni Murtagh arsenal," Frankie said. "Like it or not, Joson is going to enter the modern age."

"Such a shame," Tess said. "This is a beautiful country. It will be forever changed. And who's to say it is for the better?"

"Like you would give up your tech," Frankie said with a derisive smile.

Tess shrugged. "You Orions care about nothing but technology," she said. "There is no beauty in your souls."

Jay snorted. "Do they even have any trees left in Orion?"

"We've got trees! Tons of them!" Frankie retorted.

"But are they real?" Jay asked slyly.

They started squabbling again.

Calvin and Shane scooted closer to Jiho.

"Those guys don't believe in hocus-pocus," Calvin said. "But we do."

Shane nodded, his eyes wide with old fears. "We're from

Old Bellprix, the part that's not as modernized as our capital. They might have never seen a real monster before, but we have." He shuddered. "I once saw a neighbor who died from influenza rise up and walk the land again."

"And we've seen things that look like people kill and eat other people," Calvin said. "So when you said there are magical creatures in the forest, what we need to know is what kind of creatures are we talking about?"

Jiho sighed. "The kind that eat people."

"Crap," Calvin said.

CHAPTER 6

EARLY IN THE morning, the crew headed to their destination, southwest of Hanoe. Jiho had worried all night that he might destroy the magic spells on them if he rode one of the motorbikes. Instead, he was able to hitch a ride on a horse-drawn carriage without drawing too much attention to himself. The others had just shrugged and called him old-fashioned. But Jiho had watched wistfully as they rode out on their motorbikes. It looked like fun.

The caravan took a couple of hours to get to their base camp. Jiho had wondered why they had chosen this part of the Kidahara, but now he understood. They were in a part of the woods that was open, with wide spaces for passage. The camp faced the tall, dense, closed canopy tree line that would lead to the heart of the forest. Jiho remembered the map he had seen at the foreman's tent. This was the straightest point to Mount Jiri. Despite all the elaborate plans for building cities in the Kidahara, the end game seemed to be Mount Jiri. Jiho wondered why the Orions were so intent on getting to the volcano. No humans had ever gotten to the mountain, as far as he knew. At least none who ever returned alive.

At the edge of the forest, the foreman gathered all the workers.

"All right, people, here's where the job starts," he said, his cigar clamped firmly between his teeth. "We chop down every tree to form a nice wide path from here until we reach the edge of the mountain. And then we're going to level that thing down to a pile of rubble."

Of all the mountains of the Kidahara forest, the largest and oldest was Mount Jiri. The last time the volcano had erupted was five hundred years ago.

This was not right. Jiho could no longer ignore the unease that crept up his spine and lodged into his throat. This went far beyond clearing the trees of Kidahara. Destroying the mountains would violate all the natural laws. A shiver went through him. He feared what would happen if the magical creatures of Kidahara learned of the Omni Murtagh plans. He feared that none of these crewmen would manage to come out alive.

It was Jiho's crew's job to scout the area beforehand, to mark the trees that were valuable for lumber and make sure nothing dangerous was lurking. But soon the foreman changed his mind. The earlier crew had begun clearing the trees with loud buzz saws, but none of the saws lasted for more than a minute.

Nelson cursed at the wasted expense of magic spells that didn't work. They would have to do it the old-fashioned way. And because time was short, and without the buzz saws it would take them ten times longer, Jiho's entire crew was given axes and told to chop down trees.

Jiho held the heavy ax in his hand and lined up with Calvin, Shane, and Frankie in front of a group of trees. He stared hard at the ax. He'd never cut down a tree before. He was too young when his father was around. Once his father left, Jiho had avoided the forest. His uncle took down trees only when absolutely necessary and never from the Kidahara.

To the right, they could hear the clatter of falling trees as groups of men took down the bamboo grove.

"Come on, Jiho, you take the first whack," Frankie said. "These trees ain't that big. You can take it down yourself."

Jiho gazed at the tall maple tree before him. It was sick and diseased. He could tell by the way it listed to the left, its roots lifting out of the soil, and the base covered in large mushrooms. If he were to hazard a guess, he'd say an oni came by and knocked into the tree, causing it to uproot. It had probably been slowly starving to death for months.

Saying a quick prayer to the tree, Jiho slammed his ax

into the thick trunk. The tree shuddered as if in agonizing pain. Jiho froze in place, his eyes glued to the tree. He saw a yellowish smoke seep out of the gash and pull together into a small form, no bigger than a child. It floated toward him, and then he was completely enveloped in it. Gasping, he fell to the ground suddenly and then watched as the figure disappeared into the sky. He was shaking so bad he couldn't stand up. The spirit of the tree had thanked him for its release, but it had also passed on a warning. He saw a vision of blood and death—the kingdom of Joson overrun with all that was evil in the Kidahara.

"What the hell was that thing?" Shane asked. All three boys were staring down at Jiho with looks of concern and nervousness.

"It looked like a ghost," Shane said.

"Ain't no such thing," Frankie snapped. He nudged Calvin. "You didn't see nothing like that, right?"

Calvin was quiet, only gazing somberly at the tree.

"Get up, boy! You take that tree down now, if you know what's good for you," the foreman shouted as he came stomping over to them. The other boys backed away as Jiho got up onto his shaking feet. He forced the vision away. It wasn't real. There was nothing to fear. The Orion men were well prepared for any and all dangers. They could handle the monsters of the Kidahara. Jiho pushed away the niggling doubt in his mind and took a deep breath. He pulled the ax out of the tree and began to chop in earnest. After an extended period of feverish action, he felt the tree starting to give way.

"Timber!" Frankie shouted.

Jiho looked curiously at Shane. "That's what the Orioners say when a tree is falling," Shane explained.

The tree fell with a crash, and immediately a group of men came over to haul it away.

Jiho wiped the sweat from his forehead and looked around at the others. Some of the crews had already downed their trees, while others were still working on them. These trees were smaller and slimmer. But he worried about how they would take down the older, larger trees in the forest. They would need a lot of men to chop one down.

And what would the spirits do?

This was a good question. It had been years since he watched his father cut down trees in the forest. Nothing bad had ever happened, but his mind was full of his father's warnings.

Never take the life of a tree unless you absolutely have to.

Jiho shook his head hard. No. It was time for change. They couldn't live in fear anymore. The trees had to be cleared. The creatures of the Kidahara had to be wiped out.

And the mountain? What will you do when they reach them?

Jiho could feel the hairs on his arm rising with his goose bumps. The mountains were sacred. How could they even think of touching them? He shivered.

By the third day, the team was farther into the forest. They'd cut down a large, wide path through the heart of the Kidahara, but Jiho could feel the hopelessness of the undertaking. The Kidahara was too big. Even the hundreds of men Omni Murtagh had brought were not enough for the job.

Also, Jiho had noticed the singular lack of the Kidahara's magical creatures in their path. But he felt the sensation of being watched.

They're waiting.

Jiho tried to wave away the thought, but it was too troubling. They were all out there watching them. Waiting to see what all these humans were doing in their forest. Jiho became so spooked at the idea, he knew he had to do something. He had to leave the forest. He went in search of the foreman.

"We need more men," he heard the foreman complaining to Brock Murtagh. "This would have been fine if our chain saws and bulldozers worked, but the only thing we can bring into this damn forest are the axes. It'll take us a thousand years at this rate."

"Your job is to clear a pathway to the base of the mountain, not take out the entire forest," Murtagh said. "I want you to do your job so that my men can blast that bloody mountain into a crater."

Murtagh walked away abruptly, leaving the foreman angrily chomping on his pipe.

"Mr. Nelson . . ." Jiho approached.

"What do you want?" the foreman snapped. He didn't even pretend to be nice anymore.

"Well, I think I have to go home now. I was wondering if I can get paid for my days here," he asked.

The foreman glared at Jiho. "Now, you listen here, kid! You've been hired for this project, and you don't get paid until it's done. You read me?"

Jiho didn't know what reading had to do with getting paid, but he nodded. He had no choice. He had to stay. His family needed the money.

Two days later, Jiho's friends were broken into smaller groups. Frankie was now teamed up with the Urcian girls Tess and Jay, and the three Quest-playing boys were officially their own team.

Calvin shook his head. "I don't know what the foreman was thinking with those teams. Frankie will spend the whole time arguing with the Urcians, and the Quest boys will spend every moment trying to trade their cards and forget to take down any trees."

"Guess we'll have to show them how it's done!" Shane said.

Jiho smiled weakly. The farther into the Kidahara they ventured, the more uneasy he became.

Later that afternoon, what Jiho had feared from the first moment he entered the forest finally happened. He and his small crew stood before a large tree that he knew he couldn't touch. It was a deep, instinctive knowledge that could not be explained. His father would examine the trees, smell them, pray over them, before even touching them. But this tree needed no such ritual. It reeked of malevolent energy. Jiho wanted to get as far away from it as he could. This was a bad tree.

But who would listen to him? The foreman would scream and hurl insults. All he cared about was clearing as much of the forest as they could. Jiho needed to get away from the tree.

"This tree is going to be very difficult," Jiho said. "Let's take down that one instead."

He pointed to a smaller tree several meters away and quickly started walking. He didn't give anyone else a chance to argue. Jiho heaved a relieved sigh when they followed him without question. While Calvin had looked at him curiously, Shane didn't seem to care.

Just then, the foreman walked by and stopped in front of the evil tree. He pivoted angrily, glaring at everyone. Jiho dropped his head, avoiding the foreman's eyes.

"Calvin, get your crew up here and take down this tree," Nelson shouted.

Jiho looked up in alarm as he watched his friends walk back to the tree.

"No! Don't touch it!" Jiho shouted. He ran forward and put a hand on Calvin's chopping arm. "This tree is ancient and has a magical creature tied to it. If you cut it down, you will bring a curse onto you. Onto all of us!"

"What the hell are you doing, kid?" The foreman came rushing over and smacked Jiho hard on the back of his head.

"Cut down this tree right now!" he shouted at Calvin.

But Calvin's face had turned ashen. Lowering his ax, he shook his head. "No, sir, not that one. It's got a face like a man on it!"

He was right—in the very center of the tree, a face had appeared. Somewhat humanlike, but grotesque and frightening. At the same time, the sky above them turned black as large clouds blocked the sunlight. It was now as dark as night. Jiho's stomach twisted and turned in warning. Something bad was going to happen. He could feel it, but he didn't know how to stop it.

"You fools!" the foreman shouted. "I'm not going to let a few scary stories slow down my schedule." He grabbed the ax from Calvin's limp hands and swung it hard, right into the middle of the face.

A piercing shriek filled the air, so loud the men bent over in pain as they tried to cover their ears. Where the ax lay buried within the tree, a black substance seeped out, flowing and amorphous as it began to take shape. The foreman tried to release the ax, but he couldn't. He was stuck fast to the handle.

"Help! Somebody pull me off this thing! Quickly!"

Several men ran forward to help the foreman, but they too were stuck tight to wherever they touched. And the black matter had now taken shape, into a creature like nothing any of them had ever seen before. It was tall, with heavy, long black fur that covered its entire body, but its face had no eyes or nose. Only two slits for nostrils and a large, gaping mouth filled with razor-sharp teeth. All the men were screaming as the creature began to move toward them.

"What the hell is that thing?" Calvin had gripped Jiho's shoulder tight as all the boys scrambled away.

"It's a nightwalker," Jiho whispered. "A man-eater. It can't see, but it has incredibly sharp hearing and sense of smell."

Calvin stepped forward. "We have to help them."

"No," Jiho said sharply, lunging for his friend and pulling him back. "It's too late. If you touch them, you'll get stuck too. We have to get out of here."

Suddenly, from the other side of the tree, another nightwalker began to take shape.

"Now would be a good time to run," Jiho stuttered.

"Everybody, get the hell out of here!" Calvin shouted. "Those things are flesh-eaters!"

Immediately, panic ensued as everyone ran for their lives, and the screams of the men stuck to the ax chased them deep into the woods.

Jiho and his friends followed a group of Orion men who were heading down the clear-cut land back toward base camp. They could see the outlines of the trucks when Jiho felt the sharp pain in his gut that told him danger was close by. Unsure of where it was coming from, he slowed down and grabbed hold of Calvin and Shane by the arms.

"Jiho, we have to get out of here!" Shane tried to pull away, but Calvin stopped.

"What is it, Jiho?"

"Don't move," he whispered.

Suddenly, a pack of red-skinned, horned onis stepped out from the forest, holding huge iron clubs. The lead oni grabbed a man in the front of their group and stuffed him into his mouth, as the man's screams rang out.

Shocked and scared, they all scattered. Jiho, Calvin, and Shane cut into the uncleared forest and ran west, away from the onis and the nightwalkers.

They ran for what felt like hours, before finally coming to a halt. There was no one else around. They'd lost all the other workers.

"Hey, Jiho, is it safe? Do you know the way back into town?" Calvin asked.

Jiho didn't answer right away. The darkness had obscured just about everything, and it was impossible to figure out where they were.

"He's lost," Shane responded. "It's so dark. Let's light a fire and make camp."

"No," Jiho said sharply. "It's too dangerous."

He looked up into the trees, analyzing which ones looked the strongest and the safest.

"This one." He pointed at the tallest and biggest of the trees, with large swooping branches. "We need to climb up those branches and go as high as we can in order to make it through the night."

The other two boys looked up at the tree and gulped. "You sure about this, Jiho?"

Jiho nodded. "We haven't seen the worst of the Kidahara monsters yet. And fire will attract them. We need to hide for now and stay quiet until the sun comes up."

Shane looked uneasy. "Jiho, that monster came right out of the tree. How do we know we won't get eaten while we sleep?"

"This tree is safe," Jiho said with assurance. "I promise we'll be safer up here than anywhere else."

Calvin nodded grimly. "Let's do it."

All three of them began to climb. About halfway up, they each tested their weight on a branch before choosing one for the night. Calvin's branch was lower than the others, because he was bigger and heavier.

"You think I'll be okay here?" he asked.

Jiho tempered his impulse to climb higher and chose the branch right above his friend. "Yeah, just be real quiet," he said. "You still have your rope, right?"

Calvin and Shane nodded and tied themselves onto their

branches. Once he saw his friends were secure, Jiho did the same. He leaned his head against the tree trunk and closed his eyes, exhausted. But sleep was elusive. The noises of the forest were magnified, and everything sounded like the footsteps of a monster creeping around them, looking for its next meal.

The last vision that Jiho saw as he fell asleep was the sight of the nightwalker's grotesque face as it attacked the men.

The early rays of the rising sun woke Jiho from his fitful sleep. He untied himself and immediately looked to check on the others. Shane was still passed out to his right. He looked down and found Calvin staring up at him with alert eyes.

"Did you sleep at all?" he whispered.

Calvin shook his head. "Not after the one really big thing that passed in the middle of the night. What was it? I thought we were going to get shaken out of our tree."

"That was an oni," Jiho said. "Like the ones we saw yesterday."

"But the one last night wasn't red," Calvin said. "It had yellow skin that glowed in the dark."

"Yeah, onis come in all different colors. Like flowers. But unlike flowers, they have a revolting smell and will eat you."

"And the hairy black things that came out of the tree? They eat you too?"

Jiho nodded. "But we were really lucky we didn't see any

Agma. They're demons of the underworld that resurrect from the bodies of those who died violently. If they don't eat you, they turn you into one of them."

"Like zombies," Calvin said with a shudder. "What doesn't eat you in this crazy place?"

"Well, the namushin are peaceful tree spirits and only eat the fruit of the trees—"

"It's okay, Jiho," Calvin interrupted with a tired smile. "It was a rhetorical question."

"Ah," Jiho replied. "Sorry you couldn't sleep."

Calvin shook his head. "Who could after all that happened yesterday? I can sleep as much as I want when we're out of this forest. Right now, I just want to survive."

They were quiet for a moment before Calvin cleared his throat.

"Jiho, how did you know those onis were going to step out of the forest like that?"

"I don't really know," Jiho said. "I think it's related to the fact that magic doesn't work on me. I can sense strong magic around me. And if it's dangerous, my stomach actually starts to hurt."

"Whoa, that's a really good gift to have in this place," Calvin said. "I'm sure glad we're friends. You saved our lives."

"I'm glad we're friends too," Jiho replied.

Shane let out a loud snore.

"Good thing he didn't do that last night . . . ," Calvin

said. "Otherwise I would've pushed him out of the tree."

Jiho looked over to where Shane lay contorted against the tree trunk. At some point during the night, Shane had twisted his body around so he could wrap his arms around the tree trunk, his face smashed against the bark.

"How does he sleep like that?" Jiho marveled.

"Shane can sleep standing up in the rain if he's tired," Calvin said. "Come on, let's wake him."

Jiho grabbed a handful of nuts from his branch and flung them at Shane.

"Ow!" Shane woke up with a start.

"We're getting out of here," Jiho said.

"Now, that's what I'm talking about!" Shane said fervently as he untied himself from his branch.

Sometimes Jiho wondered if the universal translator had a glitch in it as he puzzled over the meaning of his friends' words. Shane hadn't been talking at all. He'd been sound asleep.

Down on the ground, the boys debated which way to go.

"If we head back toward camp, we can see who is still around and hopefully get some grub," Calvin said.

"Dude, are you out of your mind?" Shane yelled. "Did you see that thing that ate the foreman? ATE HIM?! There's no way I'm going anywhere near that thing. If camp is that way, then I'm going in the absolute opposite direction."

"That would take you even farther into Kidahara Wilderness," Jiho said. "I actually think Calvin's idea is a good one. The nightwalker can't exist in the sunlight, so we will definitely be safe from it now."

"Well, why didn't you say that in the first place?" Shane asked. "Let's go, I'm starving."

What had seemed like hours of travel in the dark of the night only took them forty minutes in daylight with Jiho's trusty old compass. They passed the tree-clearing site first. There were no remnants of the massacre from the night before. No way to know how many people were killed. Jiho found himself drawn back to the nightwalker tree. The grotesque face that had been there before was now gone. The only thing that remained was the large gouge mark where the foreman had plunged his ax into it. He reached his arm out, wanting to touch the tree, when a hand shot out and stopped him.

"Don't do that, Jiho," Calvin said, shaking his head. "That's a bad idea."

Jiho snatched his hand back and nodded. "I don't know what came over me."

The boys kept walking and reached base camp quickly. The camp was deserted. As Calvin and Shane scavenged for food, Jiho found the foreman's tent. The map of Kidahara was still there, the forest marked in red, like the blood of all the men who had died.

Jiho remembered the monk's words. *Foolish men. They know not what they will unleash.*

The truth was, they never had a chance. And that is

what always happened when humans underestimate the Kidahara.

Stepping out of the tent, he saw that Calvin and Shane had three backpacks filled with food and necessities. They each carried one of the weapons called rifles. Shane handed Jiho a backpack, a water canteen, and a sword.

"I know you don't like our rifles, but you're gonna need a weapon to get out of here," Shane said. "I figured a sword would be more your speed."

"Speed?" Jiho was confused.

"He means more your style," Calvin answered patiently.

"Ah." Jiho nodded. "Thank you." He wondered if he should tell them that he didn't know how to use a sword either.

"Let's get out of here," Shane said. "This place gives me the heebie-jeebies."

The translator beeped at the untranslatable words. "The what?" Jiho asked.

"You know, the chills. Goose bumps."

Before Jiho could respond, his attention was distracted by the rustling of leaves.

Calvin and Shane raised their weapons.

Out of the bushes came Frankie, Tess, and Jay.

"Calvin! Shane! You're alive!" Frankie looked like he was on the verge of tears, he was so relieved to see them. The other two looked shell-shocked. The three sat heavily on the ground, exhaustion on their faces.

"We're so glad to see you all," Calvin said. "But where are the others?"

"We lost Mac, Buddy, and Gabriel." Frankie's face was grim. "They were . . . they were . . ." He choked up and couldn't speak.

"They're dead," Jay said flatly. "We took turns keeping watch around the campfire. Mac and Buddy took the first shift. We don't even know what took them. One minute they were there and the next they were completely gone. Gabriel ran away. All we found was his bloody shoe with his foot still in it."

"The fire was a bad idea," Tess said. "It was like a beacon attracting the monsters to us. We left it and ran. We've been running ever since."

There was a moment of silence as they all thought of their lost friends.

"We need to get out of here quick. Let's see if any of our bikes are still working," Calvin said.

They walked to where they'd left their bikes, only to see that everything had been destroyed.

"Looks like we're gonna have to walk," Calvin said grimly.

Jiho looked up at the sky to see the position of the sun. "We need to get out of the forest while it's still bright. I don't know if we can survive another night here."

"Hey, you guys," Shane said in a weird voice. "Wasn't there a path out of here when we arrived?"

"Yeah. Why?"

"Because the trees have surrounded us."

Alarmed, Jiho ran to the edge of the base camp and walked the entire perimeter in disbelief. Shane was right. The forest had taken the path from them.

CHAPTER 7

THE BOTAN CLAN had always lived on the outskirts of the Kidahara, where the peonies grew wild and lush. Their clan insignia was the white peony. They were traders on paper but bandits in real life. They traded the herbs and roots of the Kidahara, which were highly coveted by both magical and nonmagical folks. There were two types of ginseng, the regular kind that grew wild along the mountainside and was used for health tonics, and the special ginseng that had wrinkled old-men faces, which witches and wizards used for antiaging and beauty spells. Delicious curly bracken fiddlehead ferns that were coveted by both cooks and witch doctors alike. Black hoof mushrooms that good witches used for medicinal purposes and bad witches used for poisonous ones. And mugwort for enchantments.

They stole only from the indolent wealthy and indiscriminately shared their bounty with all who were in need. The Botan clan knew to grease the palms of the magistrates and soldiers, who then turned a blind eye to their crimes. That had always been their way. Until the Orions came with Prince Roku, and foreign mercenaries and soldiers flooded the Joson roads.

Each matriarchal leader in the Botan clan was referred to as the White Peony. Even though Micah had an older brother, Kai, it was Micah who was the clan leader. She inherited the role at the death of her mother five years ago, when she had been only eleven. It was after her mother had tried to commune with the moonstone. Micah's mother got sick, her mind wandering at times. She became feverish and would yell loudly at an unseen person, raging at them, telling them that they could never possess her. The clan doctor said it was a sickness attached to the moonstone. That it was evil and should be destroyed. But Micah's mother wouldn't let anyone touch it. The moonstone had been with the clan for centuries, and there had never been any problems with it, until a month before the chief died, when it began to glow.

There was no doubt in anyone's mind that the moonstone had killed Micah's mother. From the moment it glowed and the chief tried to commune with it, the moonstone took control of her mind, wasting her away.

When Micah became the White Peony, she also came

into possession of the moonstone. The clan elders urged her to destroy it, but Micah couldn't bear to part with it. She was both fascinated and repulsed by the object. It was responsible for the death of her mother, and yet Micah coveted it. Disgusted and angry, she had the glowing stone placed in a satin-lined iron box and locked away.

A few years passed before she was able to look at the stone again. The Botan clan was hit hard by the entry of the Orion teams, with their battalions that patrolled the roadways of Joson and made it hard to continue the clan's way of life. And their clan had always relied on the safety of the Kidahara to protect them from retribution. They knew where to camp safely from the dangerous creatures and hide from soldiers unaware of the reputation of the forest. And yet the Orion kept trying to build their roads into it.

Nothing was safe or sacred anymore. Micah's clan was suffering, and something had to be done. But still the moonstone called to her. Micah knew it was magical, and she was determined to learn its magic.

"Don't touch it, Micah. It destroyed your mother. I can't let it destroy you also," Mari said. She was the Botan clan's first command, and Micah's mother's partner ever since Micah was little. Given Mari's long-standing role as a second mother to Micah, she didn't call her White Peony. Not yet, anyway. The loss was still too raw.

"We should sell it," Kai said. "I bet we could get a fortune for it in town."

Micah refused. The moonstone had been with the clan for so long.

She rationalized her fascination with the moonstone by convincing herself that she was different from her mother. Her mother always said Micah was the smart one. And Micah had the ability to wield some magic, unlike her mother. Whatever it was in the moonstone that had driven her mother mad, she was sure it would not do the same to her.

But when she tried to sense the magic in the stone, she was shocked at its overpowering strength. Immediately, Micah realized she wasn't strong enough to use it and quickly locked it back in its box. But the damage was done. Soon after, the dreams started. Dreams of the end of the world: the Kidahara on fire and her entire clan dying. She would wake up in a cold sweat every night. Were these just nightmares or were they foretellings of a dark future?

Micah started to believe that her nightmares might actually be prophecies when the Botan clan's way of life took a drastic change for the worst.

For years the Botan clan had hampered the Orions from making their way through the Kidahara, but now with Prince Roku's blessing, the Orion soldiers were everywhere. And Micah had heard rumblings that a political coup was happening. Prince Roku was planning to take over the palace.

If that happened, then nothing would stop the destruction

of the Kidahara. If the Kidahara was destroyed, their world would change completely. The Botan clan would not survive. Micah knew that it was her duty to all her ancestors to protect her clan.

She knew she needed advice and decided to seek out the ancient sea hag. Taking only her closest guards and Mari, Micah left the clan in the hands of her aunt Sirus, a seasoned warrior and skilled adviser. The sea hag lived on a remote island off the southern shores of Joson. It was a week's ride by horseback, and then they would have to find a fisherman willing to take them to and from the sea hag's island. Micah brought several pounds of their priceless wild ginseng. And yet it took nearly all of it to bribe a fisherman to take them.

On the island, they found the sea hag's decrepit shack and waited for her arrival from the sea at sunset.

"Do not look at the sea hag until she greets you," Mari warned. "If you see her while she is transforming, she'll eat your still-beating heart right out of your chest."

As soon as the last ray of the sun disappeared, they heard the dragging footsteps of a large creature approaching the shack. Micah and her clan members respectfully kept their eyes on the ground. When the sea hag entered, Micah caught the shadow of a grotesque form in the light of the full moon. It had tentacles and claws, and the intense brackish smell of the sea filled the room.

"Who are you and what do you want?"

Taking it as a greeting, Micah faced the sea hag, barely repressing a shudder. The sea hag had the face of a monstrous old crone and a curved spine that made her look like a hunchback. Legend had it that the sea hag had once been a beautiful fairy creature who had loved and lost a fisherman to the seventh daughter of the dragon king, who lived deep in the sea. Heartbroken, she had pledged to search for her love in every part of the ocean. She'd never found him and instead was transformed into the hideous sea creature she was now. Micah refused to believe the sea hag was ever beautiful.

Micah bowed and introduced herself.

"I knew your mother," the sea hag replied. "I can taste the delicious sadness emanating from you, so she must be dead now."

"Yes," Micah whispered. She cleared her throat. "When she died, she left me this." Micah opened the case, holding the glowing moonstone. The sea hag looked at it with an unusual expression of both fear and longing.

"Do you know what it is?"

"It's a moonstone. It is seeking its two sisters, and to return to its master," the sea hag whispered.

"Who is its master?"

The sea hag began to shake. "You must leave and take this cursed thing with you."

"Please, you have to help us."

"I said leave. Now!" The sea hag roared so loudly that the walls shook and the sky thundered.

"My apologies," Micah said with a bow. She was no wiser and more frustrated than when she arrived. Who could help her?

"What a waste of ginseng," Mari muttered as they walked back to the boat. "This proves that we must destroy it. Even the sea hag was afraid of the moonstone."

Micah didn't answer. The sea hag's fear had made Micah more determined to keep the powerful orb. She was sure it could be her clan's salvation, if only she knew how to use it.

They left the island with the very nervous fisherman and headed back home with heavy hearts. Micah could not shake the feeling of impending doom that would over-whelm her at times.

When they returned to their clan, the misfortune Micah so greatly feared had struck. Their campgrounds were cov-ered with the injured and the dead. Her people were dazed and grief-stricken.

"White Peony! Thanks to the ancestors that you are back!" an injured guard hobbled over to greet them.

"Orion soldiers attacked and overwhelmed our warriors. Your aunt Sirus is gravely hurt, and they kidnapped your brother."

Mari cursed fiercely.

"We never should have left camp," Micah whispered.

"Then the Orions would have kidnapped you instead," Mari retorted. She turned back to the guard. "What did they want?"

"Their demands don't make sense," the guard said. "They said that if we ever want to see Master Kai again, then we must find the lost princess in the Kidahara and bring her back to Prince Roku, dead or alive."

"The lost princess? What are they talking about? She died five years ago," Micah said. "And even if she managed to survive, how are we supposed to find her? People who want to disappear in the Kidahara are never found again."

"If anyone can find her, it would be the Botan clan," Mari said. "Let's help our clan members for now and talk about this later."

They spent the rest of the day caring for the injured, and burying the dead. When they were done, Micah wandered the forest alone. She needed time to clear her mind. To calm her rage. No one had seen or heard of the lost princess in years. Everyone assumed she must have died in the Kidahara. For how could a young girl have survived the most dangerous forest in the world? If Prince Roku wanted her dead or alive, it meant he was making a play for the royal throne. Which meant if the princess was still alive, she wouldn't be for long.

Micah racked her brain, trying to think of some way to bring her brother safely back without getting involved in the political corruption. She headed for the lake, where she could scream without fear of being heard.

"What is it, child, that makes you despair?"

Micah whirled around at the voice and saw a woman so

beautiful that Micah felt compelled to avert her eyes.

"Who are you?"

"I am the fairy Samena," the woman responded. "Tell me what troubles you so gravely."

Micah slowly faced the fairy again and stared wondrously into eyes as blue as the bright summer sky. Pale skin framed by hair as white as lightning. She was what Micah had always imagined an angel would look like. Beautiful in a cold, otherworldly manner. Micah was mesmerized. She found herself relaying all that had occurred since her mother's death.

"Do not be afraid," the fairy said. "I am here to help you."

"You can help me?" Micah asked. "But why?"

"Because I am your benefactor." The fairy smiled, a slight curving of her thin lips that gave no indication of warmth but was dazzling in its beauty. "I am your savior. I am your master. I will help you save your brother and your clan."

"You would do that for me?" Micah asked, her eyes locked on the fairy in utter entrancement.

"Yes, my pretty child," the fairy replied. "And in return, you will belong to me."

Micah didn't feel pretty. Her own pale skin looked sallow and her black hair so dull compared to the fairy. But when Samena gazed at her, she felt glorious. "I will be yours," Micah whispered.

As Micah pledged loyalty to this strange fairy, she could not help but wonder what price she would pay for her help.

"How will I be able to contact you?" Micah asked.

"The moonstone," Samena responded. "It is fairy magic. Touch it, and I shall hear you."

Several hours later, Micah returned to her camp. Her clansman surrounded her in deep concern.

"What will we do now?" Mari asked.

"We'll do what we have to do to get Kai back," Micah said grimly.

"What's your plan?"

"We go find the princess Koko."

"Even if Roku is sending us on a wild-goose chase?"

Micah's eyes glazed over for a moment, hearing the fairy's voice in her head, whispering of the princess and her sightings. "I believe she's alive and in the Kidahara forest. I will find her."

Micah thought of her brother once again, scared and alone in a castle prison, and her lips tightened grimly.

"Don't worry, Kai, I'll find the princess and bring her to Roku, dead or alive."

CHAPTER 8

JIHO LED THE group through the forest without any idea of where he was going. The terrain had shifted so drastically there was nothing recognizable. The team tried to follow the path that they had taken into the forest, but it was impossible to know where they were. The trees that they'd cut down had seemingly grown overnight, thicker and denser than before. None of their directional devices worked, and even Jiho could not find a way out for them. Using his senses, Jiho tried to steer his friends away from the strongest magical spots. The sun rose high above them, but a strange cool mist rose up from the grounds.

Every time he thought he knew the way out, the trail would turn in on itself and Jiho would feel lost again. It was like the forest didn't want them to leave. But Jiho wasn't about to tell the others, who were already deathly frightened. He didn't want to tell them that for the last hour he'd felt an acute sense of being watched. The only thing he knew for sure was that whoever was watching them wasn't a magical creature. He just wished he knew what they wanted.

His gut churned in a sudden warning, but it was too late. They were quickly surrounded by bandits wearing white peony insignias and holding their signature double blades in attack formation.

"Drop the bags, and you can keep your hands," the lead bandit said.

Calvin and the others immediately raised their rifles and pointed them at the bandits.

"Why don't you guys drop the knives and you can keep your heads, instead?"

The lead bandit pulled off her mask and smiled. In a sudden movement so fast it was a blur, she grabbed Frankie and held her blade to his throat.

"We seem to be at an impasse."

Jiho could feel the dangerous tension between everyone. There was deadly intent in all of their eyes.

"Listen, we don't want any harm," Jiho said. "I will trade you my bag filled with supplies for him."

The bandit sliced the other bag off Frankie's shoulders. "And this one too," she said with a half smile.

Jiho moved carefully forward, holding his bag in front of him.

"Make the wrong move and you'll be dead, thief," Calvin shouted.

"Don't underestimate the deadliness of our blades, foreigner," she retorted.

Jiho froze.

He stared at the bandit, noting the narrow, steely gaze of her dark hooded eyes and the wicked curve of her lips, as if she were perpetually sneering at life. She was the youngest and smallest of the bandits, and yet she was the most intimidating.

He turned back to look at his friends and was shocked to see that Calvin was just as fearsome.

He put up his hands in between them. "We're just going to exchange this bag for our friend," he said. "No need for anyone to die."

Jiho moved forward again with the bag outstretched and his other hand reaching for Frankie, whose blue eyes were wide, bulging frantically out of his eye sockets.

"I'm going to count to three and we'll trade, okay?"

The bandit didn't respond, keeping her unblinking gaze on him.

"One, two, three!"

The bandit grabbed the bag, and Jiho grabbed Frankie, pulling him away from the bandit. But in a split second, the bandit had Jiho in her grasp instead.

"And now we'll be taking the rest of the bags too, foreigner."

"No good, rotten liars!" Calvin growled. "You let him go, or we'll shoot you all down!"

But before she could respond, Jiho put out his arms, in warning. "I'm afraid we are all gonna be dead if we stay here. Something bad is coming."

CHAPTER 9

THE HAIR ON the back of his neck tingled and his nose twitched as he sensed the oncoming danger heading toward them. The trees suddenly shook and the ground shuddered below them.

"Fall back!" the bandit leader ordered and the bandits vanished into the brush. As the Botan clan members disappeared, Jiho thought he saw the flash of a hooded figure, a woman with white hair he'd seen before.

Before he could think of who she was, a foul odor caused him to gag. He turned to face the largest and most frightening oni he'd ever seen, holding a massive iron club.

"Do not run, little humans. For I am hungry and will get angry if you run."

For a moment they all stood frozen as the oni slowly approached.

"Good little humans," the oni crooned as he reached toward them with a massive hand.

"*Run!*" Jiho screamed as he pushed the others.

"Now I'm angry!"

He heard the oni shout, and then the loud pounding of rapidly approaching giant feet made him nearly pee his pants.

Suddenly Shane stopped. "Why are we running? Let's take this monster down!"

They all stopped to shoot at the oni.

Ratatatatatatatat.

The oni lumbered to a halt and scratched its head as the bullets ricocheted off his skin like Ping-Pong balls.

"Stop that tickling!" he shouted.

Jiho pulled Shane back by his collar. "You're just making him madder!" he yelled. "We have to get away from it! Fast!"

With looks of horror, the team ran as quickly as they could.

"This way," a musical voice called out from a clearing to their left.

"Turn left!" Jiho shouted, as he immediately veered toward the voice, desperately trying to keep ahead of the furious oni. He could feel the heat of the oni's foul breath on his neck. "Run faster!" he shrieked.

All of a sudden, a tremendous crash sent branches and leaves flying all around them. Jiho turned his head and nearly fell over at what he saw. The oni was on the ground face-down, and a young girl was standing on its head, twisting down the top of its ear.

"How many times must I remind you that you are trespassing on sacred namushin ground? Do I have to teach you another lesson?"

"No, my lady," the oni was whining. "I'm sorry, my lady. When first I saw the humans, they were not on your land. I warned them not to run, but they didn't listen to me! It isn't my fault that I trespassed; it was the measly humans! Give them to me, and I shall punish them all for you!"

"That is a pretty clever try for an oni," she responded. "But you and you alone are at fault for trespassing. If I find you on my land again, I shall turn you into a flea and squash you beneath my feet."

The oni shuddered and cried.

"I am very sorry, my lady! I will promise never to do so again. But would it be all right if my lady were to give me just one little human? That little one over there!" The oni pointed at Jiho. "I am frightfully hungry, my lady!"

She twisted his ear harder, causing the oni to whimper.

"How dare you ask me for any favors when you are trespassing!" Her voice magically echoed and became a tremendous bellow, causing Jiho and his friends to cover their ears.

The oni begged for forgiveness until finally the girl released him, shoving him hard. The oni scrambled to his feet and ran quickly back the way he had come.

Jiho stood in openmouthed shock and admiration.

"Are you a namushin?" Jiho asked.

The girl laughed. It was the most entrancing sound he'd ever heard. It made him think of sunshine and soap bubbles.

"No, silly," she said. "I'm too big to be a namushin!"

"Then are you a fairy?"

She laughed again and shook her head. "I'm human, just like you."

Jiho blinked. "You just took down a full-grown, adult oni," he said. "And he was scared of you. No human can do that."

The girl frowned. "I'm a human." She glanced at the others and smiled, but they all shrank in fear, staying well behind Jiho.

Jiho shook his head slowly. "You even threatened to turn him into a flea. That's some serious magic. Are you a witch?"

She crossed her arms and glared at him. "I told you, I'm a human," she said. "But the namushin have always told me I have dragon's blood in me."

"Dragon's blood? Wow, that's extremely rare," Jiho said. "Dragons have been extinct for five hundred years. I think only the royal family is said to have a trace of it in their bloodline—"

Jiho's words came to an abrupt stop as he took in her long blue-black hair. He'd seen it before many times. "Holy octopus balls! You're the lost princess Koko!"

He turned to his friends in excitement. "She's the lost princess of Joson! She's been missing for five years!"

The others cautiously approached.

"That's right, I heard about her," Calvin said.

"I've never seen a real live princess before," Frankie said admiringly.

She stilled at his words, a sad expression on her pretty face as her eyes lost focus. "Princess Koko," she whispered. "Yes, that's me."

"The queen and king have never stopped looking for you," Jiho said.

Koko's face crumpled. "Oh, Mama, I miss my mama!"

She squatted and began to sob loudly.

At her cries, little tree creatures came crawling out of the forest and surrounded Koko, humming an intricate melody. "Namushin," Jiho whispered in amazement.

Frankie screamed in shock, trying to climb onto Calvin's back for safety, while the others gaped at the little creatures in awe. But the little namushin ignored them and instead gathered around the lost princess, comforting her.

Koko hiccupped as she wiped her face and calmed down.

She then popped back onto her feet, her crying jag completely forgotten.

"I must go," she said. "There's much to be done."

"Wait, what about us?" Jiho asked.

"What about what?"

"Aren't you going to help us?"

"What do you want?"

"We want to get out of the forest."

"Oh, I'm not leaving the forest," Koko said. "This is my home."

"But you can't just leave us!"

"Then come with me," she said. "You'll be safer with me than on your own."

Jiho turned to his friends.

They looked at the princess and the namushin and then all nodded.

"We're going with her," Calvin said.

CHAPTER 10

MICAH AND HER team watched closely from their hiding spot as the foreigners followed the lost princess. When the oni had attacked, the Botan clan did what they did best—they camouflaged themselves into the fabric of the forest and then tracked their prey.

"So the princess is alive," Mari said. "But she took down an oni single-handedly. That's some powerful magic."

Micah ignored her and concentrated on the princess. They followed and watched as the princess and the foreigners disappeared into the borders of Nackwon.

"They've gone into the Nackwon. How are we supposed to capture her when we can't go in there?" Mari was exasperated.

"Quit complaining. At least she isn't dead," Micah retorted.

"So what's our next step?"

"We need something to make the princess trust us," Micah said. "In order to do that, we have to go to the royal palace to find it."

"And how are we supposed to gain access to the palace?"

"We meet with Prince Roku, tell him what we've seen so far. Make sure Kai is okay."

"And then while we're in the palace, find something that belonged to the royal family," Mari concluded. "Nice plan, little chief."

Micah was startled to hear Mari call her that. "Little chief?" she asked.

Mari smiled. "You're beginning to impress me."

Micah and her team traveled to Jinju, the capital of Joson, where they found things had changed drastically since Prince Roku's arrival. The streets were now heavily patrolled by Orion soldiers, and the royal palace guards were wearing Orion's colors.

"We have to find out where Kai is," Micah demanded of her team. "We have to make sure he's safe first."

They all fanned out, spying on the palace, seeking out those who might give them information.

Micah soon discovered that the city was in chaos—Prince

Roku had staged a coup and imprisoned the king and queen and anyone who was loyal to them. Roku crowned himself king of Joson. The townspeople were outraged. They knew that the true power came from Orion, who'd always wanted to take over Joson. With Roku on the throne, a foreign power was now in control of their kingdom. And everyone feared the wrath of the Orion soldiers.

"Micah, your brother is being imprisoned in the dungeon. Next to the king and queen," Mari reported back. "They seem okay for now. But the conditions are bad down there."

Relieved, Micah closed her eyes and prayed that her brother would stay strong until he could be rescued.

"I know what to do," Micah said.

That night, Micah went to the palace gate, gave her clan insignia stamp—a white peony, to verify her identity—and asked for an audience with Roku. After a long wait, she was escorted inside.

Heavily armed guards checked her for weapons and manacled her hands before taking her to see the prince.

Inside his receiving room, several people sat on cushions on the floor around the prince, who lounged on a throne of satin pillows. Dancers and musicians performed in front of the inattentive audience. They were too busy trying to catch the prince's favor as he sat staring intently out the window. The room opened up onto a large terrace that overlooked the Kidahara and provided a panoramic view of Mount Jiri in the distance. The volcano was enormous and could be seen clearly from the castle. It had been dormant for over five hundred years. But it still appeared as if it could erupt at any moment.

The guard approached the prince and bowed. Only then did Roku turn his attention to them. Micah was surprised to find Prince Roku to be a very attractive young man. He was more pretty than handsome, but his eyes were as cold as the harshest winter and his thin lips curved into a cruel smile. Micah felt humiliated to be brought in front of his elegant company in chains and manacles. Hate and anger warred inside of her.

"Well, well, well, I hear the Botan clan are the only people who can find anything in the Kidahara," Prince Roku said. "I hope you have good news for me?"

Micah nodded. "I have found her. But in order to bring her to you, I need something of hers. Something to make her trust me."

"Excellent! I'll have my men take you to the princess's quarters so you can find whatever it is you need. But know this: if you fail, your brother will remain in my dungeon forever, unless I decide to take his head instead."

Enraged, Micah lunged at the prince, but was savagely restrained by the soldiers.

"If you harm a single hair on his head, I will have my revenge on you!"

Prince Roku laughed. "Such bravado. I don't know if I should be offended or amused."

He stared at her for a long moment, a sneer across his

face. "But I find it amusing right now. So I'll let you go with a warning."

The soldiers took her upstairs to the royal suites. They unlocked the door to Princess Koko's room and watched as she looked around. The curtains were drawn and the room was slightly dusty, but Micah was struck by how carefully the room had been preserved for five years. Until the queen was imprisoned, she'd kept Koko's room just as the princess had left it, waiting for her return.

A guard opened up the curtains to let in sunlight. "Don't even think of stealing anything, girl," one of the soldiers said. "Everything is inventoried."

Micah ignored him as she looked for something that the princess would recognize. Something small, something sentimental. Her gaze landed on the vanity. There was a butterfly comb that she remembered seeing in a portrait. It had adorned the princess Koko's hair. She grabbed it and showed the guard.

"I'll take this," Micah said.

The soldier snatched the pin from her hand and examined it contemptuously before finally giving it back.

"Make sure you don't lose it, girl," he sneered.

Micah bit back her angry words and let them escort her out of the palace. Mari and her team stood waiting by the palace gates.

"Did you get it?" Mari asked.

Micah showed her the butterfly pin, and Mari nodded approvingly.

"Everyone knows that pin," she said. "You chose well, little chief."

Grateful for the acknowledgment, Micah gave the command for them to return once again to the Kidahara. Micah now had a plan. She knew how she would lure the princess out of Nackwon.

CHAPTER 11

JIHO AND HIS friends ventured deeper into the forest where the trees were the tallest and the biggest. Namushin of various sizes sat on tree branches and fallen logs, staring at them with the greatest of curiosity. Some were long and slender like reeds, and others were smaller and stouter. There were even some sporting flowers on their heads.

Koko gestured to a massive tree, its trunk nearly the size of a house. "This is the entrance to Nackwon."

"What is it?" Shane asked.

"It is the realm of magic," Koko answered. "Humans are not allowed to enter unless invited by a resident of the Nackwon."

Jiho's friends stared perplexed at the solid tree trunk.

"Is something supposed to happen?" Frankie asked in confusion.

"It's hard to see at first," Koko said, but stopped short when Jiho walked through the solid trunk and disappeared from view.

Jiho stuck his head back out of the tree. "What are you guys waiting for?"

"I can't believe you can see it," Koko marveled. "Humans can't see the entranceway."

Jiho shrugged and gestured for his friends to enter.

Inside the tree, they followed along a dimly lit tunnel that took them underground. Little namushin popped their heads out from rocks and under roots. At the end of the tunnel, they found themselves in a gigantic cavern that was like a busy village marketplace. Numerous stalls filled the cavern with merchants selling and trading wares and craftsmen working and chefs cooking. Toward the back of the cavern they could see the sparks of firepits and metal workers banging on their anvils. Behind them were several tunnels with gated entrances and soldiers standing guard.

The crowds were a mix of human and magical folk. Jiho gaped at the beautiful proprietress of a fabric store who was a gumiho in her human form. She didn't even bother to hide her nine red foxtails. Next door to her was a woman with elfish features weaving elaborate rugs with intricate designs that she displayed around her shop. Down another street, a frightening-looking old woman hawked roasted spider crisps, while across the way a lovely fairy displayed jewelry made from tiny imitation moonstones.

Frankie pointed to the shop owners and asked Koko, "Is she a witch, and is she a fairy?"

Koko shook her head. "You got them mixed up," she said.

"She's the witch." Koko pointed to the jewelry shop owner.

"And she's the fairy." Koko nodded in the direction of the old woman.

The heavenly smells of roasted chestnuts and sweet pies mixed with the earthiness of the cavern was overwhelming, but in a good way.

Shane tapped Jiho on the shoulder. "I'm real hungry, think we can get some food?"

Koko overheard and waved them over to a small café away from the crowds of the central market. "Granny makes the best noodle soup in Kidasan."

"Kidasan?"

"This is Kidasan Shijang, the largest underground market in Nackwon."

"Maybe the only underground market," Jiho said.

"It's so cool," Tess responded. Turning to Jay, she said, "We could explore this place for hours."

"I'll take you around first," Koko responded. "There are parts of the Kidasan that humans aren't allowed in."

Jiho glanced back at the tunnels with armed guards and wondered what they were trying to keep out or in. "Do humans who get invited in stay here forever? Are they trapped here?" Jiho asked, thinking about his father.

"Most humans who come don't leave," Koko said. "Why would they? It's so much better here."

Rapping her knuckles on the counter, she shouted. "Granny, seven house noodles please."

The kids sat in eager anticipation as Koko poured barley tea into wooden cups and passed everyone a wooden spoon and a pair of chopsticks.

"I never learned how to use your eating sticks," Frankie said. "Could I have a fork?"

Koko shook her head. "I don't think Granny has any forks."

A wizened old woman floated seven bowls of steaming hot noodle soup over to each of them. The aroma of the rich fragrant soup made them all salivate.

"No chopsticks, no food," Granny said in a husky gruff voice before turning back to the kitchen.

All but Jiho looked dismayed.

Jiho yelled out a "thank you for the meal" and began to slurp up the fat noodles with gusto.

As the others hesitated with their chopsticks, Koko let out a giggle. "Don't worry, they're charmed so you can use them."

Tess was the first to try and found the chopsticks magically helped her pick up a large bite of noodles.

"Mmmmm, wonderful . . . ," Tess muttered around her noodles.

Jay carefully watched her friend before trying it herself. Her eyes popped wide-open in delight.

"Oh man, this is the best noodle soup I've ever had!" Shane said.

"It's the only noodle soup you ever had," Calvin countered.

"And that's why it's the best!" Shane retorted.

Frankie and Jiho didn't say a word, as both were too busy slurping noodles down as fast as they could.

Granny appeared with small bowls of pickled vegetables, spicy potatoes, and marinated anchovies that floated down in front of them. Without even questioning what they were, the kids ate everything. The bowls magically refilled themselves as soon as they emptied.

Frankie soon leaned back with a happy sigh and a large belch.

"You are disgusting," Tess said.

"Pig," Jay sniffed.

"Pardon me," Frankie said. "But it was the best dang thing I've ever eaten in my entire life! I don't know what kind of weird meat was in the soup but it was real good."

"Oh, there's no meat in it," Koko said. "Granny's a vegetarian. Those were roots and mushrooms."

Frankie looked stunned and peered into his empty bowl in betrayed confusion.

"Not meat?" he whispered to himself.

"I've never eaten so many vegetables in my life," Shane said, wondering. "I guess I wouldn't mind if it all tasted like this."

"Must be magic," Calvin said.

"No magic, just seasonings," Koko replied.

Granny reappeared with a tray of desserts that included fresh fruits and little colorful rice cake balls filled with sweet red bean cream or honey or even sesame paste.

"I'm in heaven!" Frankie said as he stuffed rice cake balls into his mouth. "Granny, can I live with you?"

"No," she said as she tromped back into the kitchen.

Everyone laughed as they bickered over the last of the dessert.

After lunch, Koko led them through the Shijang market. They marveled at giants toiling over furnaces of molten lava as they created metalworks and weapons. Nearby, goblins designed elaborate jewelry and elves made intricate glasswork.

"This place is amazing!" Frankie said.

While the others marveled at all before them, Jiho turned to Koko.

"This place is great, but what are you doing here? Why don't you go home to your parents?"

Koko looked like she was going to weep again, but she controlled herself.

"I have to train," Koko said.

"Train for what?"

"I don't know yet. But whatever it is, it will be bad."

Jiho shook his head in confusion. "That doesn't make sense to me. What could be so bad?"

"Don't you know any history?"

"You mean the Great War and Empress Luzee? But she's dead, right?"

"No, she's not dead. She was locked in a prison of volcanic ash."

"Well, as good as dead," Jiho said.

Koko shook her head. "The namushin are afraid. They sense a war is coming."

The group all looked at one another in puzzlement.

Frankie burst out laughing. "There's not gonna be any war," he said. "The five kingdoms don't have no beef with each other."

Koko shook her head. "Not a human war," she said. "The dark side of the Kidahara that was defeated, along with Luzee, has been waiting to return again. And the namushin can sense that something terrible is going to happen."

"How can they possibly know? Are they psychic?" Frankie asked.

"The namushin are tree spirits. Their roots go deep into the earth and their branches high into the sky. They can sense everything that is happening in the world. They want me to be strong enough to protect the Kidahara."

"Just you?" Jiho asked.

"No, silly," she said with a laugh. "Me and my army."

Koko gestured for them to follow her, and she took them through another tunnel where gentle gusts of air would carry them up the massive tree.

Jiho balked. If the winds were magically enhanced, he would plummet down the tunnel. "Can I take the stairs?" he asked.

Koko pointed to a narrow staircase that wrapped around the inside of the tunnel and then took off with the others. Jiho sighed as he began the long walk up the tree, listening wistfully to the laughter of his friends.

The tunnel exited out of the top of the tree and onto thick billowing clouds.

"Just keep walking," Koko's voice called back to him.

Jiho followed Koko's voice and stepped out into an entire world that spread over a vast canopy of clouds. Mountains, trees, valleys—it was a floating world completely invisible from the outside. It was as if they'd stepped into another dimension.

"What is this?" Jiho asked.

"The kingdom of Mir," Koko said. "The dragon's realm."

"Are there dragons here?"

She shook her head sadly. "They've been extinct for centuries."

The kids all gawked in shock. "Dragons once lived here?"

They looked at the beautiful place and felt the ache of

loss for creatures they'd never even seen before.

Koko led them toward a large rock formation and through a curtain of green that opened onto a vast flatland filled with thousands of soldiers, both human and magic folk.

"Mir is the safest place for us to train," she said. "For it is impenetrable."

Human soldiers were congregating in large groups under flags representing all the kingdoms. Jiho and his friends were stunned to see a gathering of so many soldiers from all over the world.

"How did they get here? Why are they here?" Jiho asked.

"The namushin have called them," Koko replied. "They are tree spirits, and they are everywhere. For five years they've gathered allies to prepare."

"To prepare for what?"

"To save the world," Koko answered.

Before Jiho could ask more questions, the others yelled loudly in excitement.

"That's a Bellprix flag," Calvin exclaimed. "And that looks like my cousin Beau! I can't believe it! All these years we thought he was dead."

Calvin bolted toward the loud and raucous crowd of soldiers talking underneath the bright sky-blue flag with yellow stars.

Shane shouted, "Wait for me," and ran quickly after him.

Tess and Jay didn't hesitate and headed over to where the purple and gold flag of Urcia soared over a crowd of brightly dressed people.

But Frankie just stared at the Orion flag before turning back to Jiho and Koko. "I don't get it. Why are Orions here? Why are they fighting for you? It's unpatriotic!"

"They aren't fighting for Joson or the Kidahara. They are preparing to protect our entire world," Koko said.

"I don't understand," Frankie said. "Why didn't we know about it? Why didn't any of them come home to warn us?"

Koko gently steered him toward the Orion encampment. "Go talk to them. They will explain it to you better than I can."

They watched as Frankie joined his fellow Orions, who welcomed him warmly. Koko turned to Jiho with a smile. "Do you want to see my favorite place?"

She took him to the other side of the flatlands, where there was a large staircase built into a mountainside. They walked up the winding stairs that brought them to a hidden palace made of marble and gold.

"What is this?"

"This was the dragon queen's palace," Koko said. She pointed at the large golden doors. "Look, the double doors were large enough for Queen Nanami to enter in her dragon form, or small enough for her human form."

Koko opened the smaller doors that were set in the larger

ones. Inside, the halls were cavernous. Large enough for dragons to walk across the black-and-white-marbled floor. At the end of the hall, the rooms became human-size. An elegant and richly opulent receiving room opened to a large banquet room. Passing through the rooms, Jiho could feel the echoes of the past.

They walked up a smaller set of stairs that led to an upstairs apartment. "This is my favorite place," Koko said.

Inside the apartment was a spacious living area and bedroom decorated with rich fur rugs and the most elegant furnishings Jiho had ever seen. The living room opened onto a large terrace that overlooked all of Mir. They walked out onto the terrace and breathed in the crisp mountain air.

"It's magnificent," Jiho said.

"I bet Nanami would fly right onto this terrace when she didn't feel like seeing anyone," Koko said. "At least that's what I would do."

"Does anyone live here now?" Jiho asked.

"No," Koko said. "But the namushin keep it clean and ready. As if they think she will return one day."

"The namushin are quite interesting," Jiho said.

Koko nodded. "They're my family."

"You mean they stole you from your family," Jiho corrected. "Your family is the king and queen of Joson. You are our princess. They stole you away and brought you to a world that is extinct. It's too weird."

Koko was quiet. "They brought me here because they

say I'm related to Queen Nanami. I have dragon's blood in me."

"But that's no reason to kidnap you."

"I know that's what it looks like, but they really are my family. And they need me."

Jiho threw his hands up. "I don't understand any of this. Why did they take you away?"

Before Koko could respond, a dozen or so namushin appeared before them and began to make a rustling and murmuring noise.

Koko listened intently before turning to Jiho. "Ask your questions later," she said. "Right now we are being summoned."

"We?" Jiho asked in surprise.

"It seems they were expecting you," Koko said. "And they are quite happy about it."

"They know who I am?"

Koko didn't answer and instead followed the namushin out of the palace.

"Come quick." She gestured to Jiho, standing by a palace door. "This is a portal door. It will take us to the other side."

She opened the door and tried to bring Jiho in, but nothing happened.

"What's happening?" she asked, puzzled. After she released Jiho's arm, the portal door revealed the other side of the realm, but when Koko grabbed Jiho's arm again, it became a solid wall.

"It's me," Jiho said. "I cancel magic. It's why I could see the entranceway to Nackwon. Magic doesn't work on me."

Surprised, Koko was about to say something when the namushin murmured loudly.

"Well, we'd better hurry, since we're going to have to go the long way."

CHAPTER 12

THEY RAN BACK down the mountain staircase to the training grounds, and then to another winding path where more namushin were waiting for them. They were led up a rocky terrain that opened onto a breathtaking waterfall that was both tall and narrow. In the foreground, a group of five large crystal chairs were placed in a semicircle that sparkled against the splendor of the natural world. Only four of the chairs were filled. The one at the end was empty. In the middle sat an elegant woman with a medium brown complexion who appeared ageless and formidable. She held a large ivory staff decorated with leaves and flowers in one hand. There was no doubt in Jiho's mind that this woman was in charge.

He was surprised to see his Orion friends there. They looked relieved to see him and just as mystified as he was.

"Welcome to Dragon Tears Waterfall," the elegant woman said in her low, melodious voice. "The Nackwon Council is grateful to have all of you join us this morning. I am Grand Council Master Aeria and these are my fellow masters, representing all of Nackwon. Master Diana of the fairy court representing the magic realm of fairy, Master Zaki of the namushin faction representing the creatures of the woodlands, and Master Remauld of the wizards and witches guild."

The masters all inclined their heads, although the jovial-looking namushin master waved his hand and smiled broadly. Master Diana was a very tall, striking-looking fairy with high, sharp cheekbones; copper-toned skin; black hair; and narrow eyes that looked nearly black and icy cold. In contrast, the diminutive Master Zaki had a warm, friendly face with big round eyes that disappeared into his chubby cheeks when he smiled. He was all green like a namushin, but was half the size of the other masters. The last master was an average-looking man with a very fair complexion and graying hair that was once a mousy brown. He would have been nondescript except for his eyes, which were a piercing blue.

Master Aeria pointed at the empty chair. "The master who represents magical creatures is no more—the chair has sat empty for five hundred years, ever since the death of the great dragon queen Nanami."

All the masters bowed their heads in respect. After a long silence, Aeria continued.

"The reason we brought you here is because we are aware of Omni Murtagh's plans to destroy the Kidahara," Aeria said. "We need you to tell us all that you can about their plan."

"We weren't really informed about it," Calvin answered. "We're just scouts."

"You all know more than you are aware of," Aeria said. "If you don't mind, would you be willing to let us retrieve the information directly?"

They all took an involuntary step back.

"Does it hurt?" Shane asked.

Aeria smiled. "No, it doesn't hurt at all. It is a simple spell that sharpens your memories and helps you remember what you've forgotten."

One by one, the Omni crew presented themselves before Aeria and their memories were retrieved.

"I remember overhearing a conversation," Calvin mentioned. "Something about Prince Roku being a principal interest holder in the Omni Murtagh company."

The council members reacted strongly. "It's as the namushin warned us. Roku is behind all of this."

"Roku is a mere human," the council master Remauld said. "What does he seek to gain from this?"

No one had an answer. They continued their memory retrieval with Frankie. "There's a map that has a detailed blueprint of a new city right at the heart of the Kidahara, where Mount Jiri is."

The masters shook their heads but moved on.

"I saw Mr. Murtagh holding a large pearly white stone. It was glowing, and I swear he was talking to it," Frankie said.

"Who is this Murtagh?" Aeria asked sharply. "And can you describe the stone?"

"He's the owner of Omni Murtagh. Well, actually the son of the owner. But he's our big boss," Calvin interrupted.

Frankie nodded. "Yeah, the stone was the size of my fist, and it was really pretty. It was the night we first entered Joson. I got up around midnight to do my business, and I saw him with the stone. I remember, 'cause it was a full moon and I thought the stone looked like a mini moon."

Master Diana grew visibly agitated. "The moonstone," she said in a shaky voice. "Then the rumors are true. She is beginning to awaken."

"We don't know that for certain," Master Zaki admonished.

"Don't be a fool, Zaki," Diana said harshly. "The signs have been all around us. We must prepare before it is too late."

"What do you mean? Who's waking up?" Frankie asked in confusion. But the council members ignored him.

"I must warn the court immediately," Diana said. She stood abruptly, gave a curt bow, and vanished.

Remauld and Zaki made elegant bows to Aeria before they too disappeared.

Aeria rose to her feet and approached the puzzled group.

"You must have so many questions," she said with a smile. "If you follow me, they will all be answered."

She walked them through a path around the waterfall, where it formed a small stream that flowed into several small pools of brilliant blue.

"This is the pool of dragon's tears," Aeria said. "It will show us the most important moments of our history."

"How does it work?"

Aeria turned to the pool.

"Great spirit, will you share with us your knowledge?"

The water began to slowly ripple, and a shadowy form could be seen deep in the depths of the pool.

"What is it you desire to know?" A deep voice rose up to them.

Aeria turned to Jiho and gestured to the pool.

"Well, I've always wanted to know how the Great War happened and why magic remains only in Joson," Jiho said.

The pool didn't respond.

"Oh," Koko said. "You have to ask it as a request."

"Great spirit, please show us how the Great War happened and why magic remains only in Joson."

The pool began to quickly share moving images on its surface. First it showed the vastness of the Kidahara, but it looked very different. It panned over open meadows and valleys and light that penetrated the entire forest. Far different from the dark, dense closed forest that it was now.

"It's like a movie," Shane said loudly, before being hushed by the others.

"Long ago, the human world and the magic world were separated by the mist of the Nackwon, which hid the magic realm within the boundaries of the Kidahara. Magical creatures stayed in the Kidahara, and humans stayed out," the spirit spoke. "But the humans began to chop down all the trees around the boundaries, angering the namushin. The namushin brought their complaint to the high court of Kidahara, a council made up of members from all the Kidahara citizens, who sent a powerful fairy, Luzee, to investigate."

The pool then showed a woman with silver hair and steel-gray eyes and skin the color of fallen snow.

"That must be Luzee before she became empress," Koko whispered.

"She was beautiful." Jiho marveled.

"She was evil," Koko replied sharply.

The pool then showed Luzee passing through a thick mist and suddenly appearing in front of a group of men who were chopping down trees. Frightened, the men attacked Luzee, who killed all of them with a wave of her hand. She ventured deeper into the human world, moving from village to village, observing human life and leaving death behind her.

"Luzee was ambitious, and she saw an opportunity to rule the human land, exploiting their fear and hatred of the unknown. Having seen the human world, she decided that she wanted it. She went to the council and advised them that the humans were a danger to the Kidahara. And then Luzee destroyed the veil that separated the two worlds. For the first time, the human world became aware of magical creatures, and they were horrified."

The next scenes showed humans waging war against dragons and other magical creatures.

"Dragons!" Frankie shouted.

"They're amazing," Jay said. "I wish we could see one for real."

No one answered. Jiho felt awful, as the spirit then shared images of humans killing dragons.

"The first dragons terrified the humans, and the humans began to hunt them down. The dragons were quick to join forces with Luzee against this new danger."

A woman wearing a black suit of armor appeared, who was more stunning than Luzee. With strong features, ebony skin and hair as blue/black as midnight that flowed down her back. She stood by Luzee's side, and the dragons that descended from the skies behind her all bowed.

"Now *she's* beautiful," Koko said. The little namushin rustled and bowed reverently at her appearance.

"She's like a goddess," Tess breathed. "Who is she?"

"The dragon queen, Nanami, in her human form. She joined forces with Luzee to stop the humans from killing dragons," Aerie said.

"Luzee used the humans' fear and tendency to violence to turn the citizens of the Kidahara against them," the spirit continued.

Behind Queen Nanami, an army of dragons rose up into the air and attacked the humans. They snatched up humans in their claws, flew high into the air, and dropped them to their deaths. Others would use their bodies to smash into soldiers. But the humans were numerous, and their weapons were deadly.

"The humans' military might was powerful, and the frightened council members of the Nackwon made Luzee their ruler. And Luzee waged war against the humans. The dark creatures of the Nackwon who feast on violence and bloodshed reveled in her leadership and quickly pledged loyalty to Luzee. With the allegiance of the dragons and the dark creatures, Luzee became all powerful, and she proclaimed herself empress of the Nackwon."

Luzee is then seen being crowned, with Nanami by her side. The next scene showed images of Luzee, leading an army of dragons and magical creatures against the humans in scenes of terrible carnage.

"But the humans invented terrible weapons that were unaffected by magic."

They saw humans rolling out cannons and using muskets and bombs that wreaked havoc on the fairy folk.

"Wait a minute, that oni we saw didn't even flinch when we shot at him," Calvin said. "He said it tickled."

"Most magical beings don't have skin like the oni, which is similar to pliable metal. Or body armor like the giant spider, the Vorax," Koko replied. "But bullets could shatter dragon scales."

The pool continued. "Angered, Luzee began to search for ways to grow her magic. She seized the precious moonstones from the fairy court and the head wizard Sejo's magic staff. And then from the dragons, she demanded a dragon's egg, the most pure magic in all the world."

"I don't understand why they would give such powerful magic to her," Jiho said.

"They had no choice," Aeria replied. "The guilds were powerless against her and her army."

"Luzee was determined to become the most powerful being in the world. She invoked the darkest magic to create the staff of ki, in an attempt to steal the power of any magical being for herself."

The water rippled as the pool showed Queen Nanami reluctantly passing a large golden egg to Luzee. The malevolent glee on the fairy's face as she gazed rapturously at the dragon's egg was frightening to behold. She then wove her magic to combine Sejo's staff with the egg and the three moonstones and a blood sacrifice. Luzee sliced her palm using a dagger with a rippled edge. She coated Sejo's staff with the black blood that oozed out of her hand. Chanting, she tossed the staff into the air as flames engulfed it, burning off the black blood and turning it pure gold. The new staff drew the dragon's egg and the three moonstones, locking them into its crown with a bright flash of light. Luzee smiled brilliantly as she seized the floating object and proclaimed it the staff of ki. The next scene showed Luzee pointing the staff at a young fairy, who was then dragged through the air into Luzee's grasp. The staff caused wisps of pink essence to float out of the fairy's mouth. Luzee inhaled the pink essence until the fairy's once-vibrant form turned limp and colorless.

"With the staff of ki, Luzee could bind any magical creature to render them powerless. She absorbed their magic by breathing in their essence and leaving them an empty, withered shell that disintegrated into dust. Luzee became so powerful that she conquered all the worlds and enslaved both human and magical creatures. But still, she was dissatisfied. She hungered for more power. She knew that dragons were the most magical beings in Nackwon. Having a dragon's egg made Luzee greedy for the power of a full dragon. So she seduced Nanami's younger brother, Koto, and while he was sleeping, she stole his magical essence. But before she could finish, Koto shifted back into his dragon form and was able to escape and warn the others. Nanami turned on Luzee and led the rebellion army against her. Humans and magical creatures worked together to fight against Luzee and her army. The knights of Joson, humans who could wield the magic that now flowed into the human world, joined forces with Nanami. But Luzee was so powerful she broke the wall between the living and the dead and brought an Agma army full of demons to our world."

The pool showed Luzee, her eyes glittering like jewels, and behind her, an army of Agma. Those who had died and become demons. Hideous and foul, Luzee unleashed the Agma on a human village. They mauled and killed the entire settlement, leaving behind new Agma to rise from the dead and join Luzee's army.

"They're zombies!" Calvin said in horror.

"*Zombie* is the human word for what they are," Aeria agreed. "They can only be completely killed by fire."

Humans and magic folk fought side by side against the Agma. Leading the charge was Nanami. This time, she wore golden armor and brandished a jeweled double-sided spear that shimmered with her every movement. Lined behind her were fire-breathing dragons and archers with flaming arrows. Nanami ordered the dragons to dive-bomb the Agma, taking out hundreds at a time.

"She's amazing," Tess said.

"When I grow up, I want to be just like her," Jay said.

"You can't," Shane retorted. "You're not a dragon."

The pool showed a much-changed Luzee, her face wild and vicious. She stared at the army of dragons streaking through the sky.

"For your betrayal, all your kind will die!" Luzee shouted as bolts of electricity ripped from her hands, directly at the attacking dragons.

The blackness of the night erupted in a dazzling light show, as spirals of electricity exploded around each dragon and they fell from the skies.

"I have killed them all," Luzee shouted maniacally. "And once I kill you, nothing will ever be able to stop me!"

"*No!*" Nanami screamed in horrified despair. Instantly, she transformed into her dragon shape, a pure midnight-black dragon, and launched herself straight at Luzee. Luzee was too slow in stopping Nanami's attack, causing a tremendous explosion upon impact. When the light faded, the two bodies were left intertwined on the ground. A Joson knight approached to examine them.

"They're still alive," he shouted.

The dragon Nanami stirred her head and whispered, "Quickly, she is too powerful to kill. We must bind Luzee before she awakens."

Using the last of her energy, she breathed her magic over the unconscious empress, binding her in an unbreakable magical cocoon with the help of the knights.

Nanami collapsed in pain. "You must promise to imprison her in the depths of Mount Jiri and protect the mountain for all eternity so that she will never be released again."

She then took hold of Luzee's staff and breathed on the large egg-like stone on top of it. The stone glowed with a bright light before fading to a pulsing shimmer. She detached the egg from the staff and handed it to the namushin who had gathered around her in grief. Nanami spoke in their whispering language. No one knew what she told them, but they broke into a mournful wail as the dragon Nanami closed her eyes and let loose her last breath.

Jiho turned to Koko and asked, "What did she say?"

"'Protect the egg,'" Koko whispered. "'For she is the last of our kind.'"

The pool faded to its depthless blue when Koko asked, "The egg. What happened to the egg?"

The crystal-blue water rippled once again into larger and larger rings, and a new vision played before her. Koko gasped to see her mother, Queen Yuna, riding in the Kidahara forest alone. She seemed lost and worried from the way she kept biting her lower lip. Suddenly, the queen reined her horse to a complete stop in front of a large pile of rocks. Her face changed to one of awe and wonder. On top of a tower of rocks was a nest, and in the nest lay a large golden egg.

"Hey! That's the egg Nanami gave Luzee," Jiho said in surprise.

The queen was so entranced that she dismounted and gathered up her skirts and began to climb. A few times she slipped, and Koko was visibly upset to see blood seep from cuts and scratches on her mom's hands and arms. But the queen was unfazed. She kept climbing until she reached the top and carefully pressed the egg against her bosom and nimbly climbed back down.

The waters rippled and the scene suddenly changed to

the queen's bedroom, where the queen held the egg to her chest and sang softly to it. The waters rippled again, showing Koko's mother sitting in a rocking chair cradling the egg, lying in bed with the egg nestled in her arms. In all ways, the queen acted as if it was a real baby. The queen sat on the rocking chair hugging the egg to her chest under the light of a full moon when it began to hatch. The queen carefully laid the egg down in a cradle next to her bed and watched as the golden shell cracked open and a tiny sparkling fist waved in the air.

Gasps of astonishment filled the air when the pool showed the next scene. Inside the egg, there was a perfectly formed baby girl with a shock of blue-black hair and a body covered in shimmering golden scales the same color as the shell. The baby's eyes were huge and black, but for the shining whites. She looked both human and completely otherworldly. The queen grabbed a wet washcloth and gently began to wipe down the baby.

"Oh!" she gasped in amazement. The golden scales fell off with every wipe. Underneath was smooth human skin. The queen gently bathed the baby until she was wiped free of all the scales.

"Koko," the queen whispered. Wrapping the little baby in a soft pink blanket, she embraced the now cooing baby. "My little Koko."

Jiho turned to peer at Koko's face as she looked at him in shock and dismay. Her black hair was the same, but her eyes were different. They were no longer deep abysses of blackness. The irises were dark brown with flecks of gold. And her skin was tanned from the sun to a golden brown, a few shades lighter than Jiho's sun-browned skin. There was no hint of the scales that once covered her entire body.

Koko turned back to the pool to see her parents, the king and queen, entranced by the baby. Jiho thought she would stare forever at the image but for the rustling and stirring of the namushin.

Wiping away her tears, she whispered, "I'm the last dragon."

Staring in amazement at the dragon princess, Jiho couldn't help but notice the look of utter devastation in Koko's eyes.

CHAPTER 13

THE REVELATIONS OF the pool were still too shocking for them to process. But Jiho worried about Koko. She hadn't said another word and had walked away in a daze, her expression blank and troubling. Jiho and the crew followed behind her as they all headed down the path.

"So she's a dragon?" Shane asked.

"She came out of an egg." Frankie shook his head. "She definitely ain't human."

"But she looks human . . . ," Shane said.

"Quiet," Tess reprimanded. "She can hear you."

"Well, I think she's amazing," Jay said.

Jiho was thoughtful. He still had so many questions to ask. He still didn't understand what the true danger was. But he could see Koko was in no condition to respond.

As they walked down the trail, a large, burly figure with a long thick walking stick stood waiting for them at the bottom of the mountain. Jiho peered in rising shock as Koko let out a cry of relief.

"Teacher!"

"Princess," the man said. "Are you all right?"

Koko nodded numbly. "I'm just tired. I need to rest."

The man bowed as Koko passed him. When he raised his head, Jiho found himself staring into his father's face. Shocked, Jiho nearly stumbled as he halted in his tracks. His father's eyes widened, and then a huge smile creased his handsome face.

"Jiho, my boy! I can't believe it's you!"

Neither could Jiho. Anger and bitterness filled him. The princess had referred to his father as "teacher." He finally knew the reason why his father had left his family five years ago. But the hurt and anger were overwhelming.

He was silent as his friends eyed them before following Koko. When they were alone, he glared at his father.

"What are you doing here?" Jiho asked.

"I was called here by the namushin," his father replied. "It was my job to teach the princess all about the Kidahara, keep her safe, and help her raise a loyal army."

"So that's why you deserted us," Jiho said.

His father lowered his eyes in shame. "I was not a good father, Jiho. I knew that your uncle and aunt would take better care of you and the girls than I ever could. So I had to go where I was needed."

"You didn't have to go, you chose to go," Jiho said sharply. "You were our father. We needed you, and you deserted us."

"Yes, I did," his father said regretfully. "And for that I am so sorry. How are your sisters?"

"You lost your right to ask that question," Jiho said bitterly.

His father winced. "Yes, I know. Living without your mother was too hard for me. So when the namushin came for me, I left without a second thought. I relied on your uncle and aunt to take care of you—I abandoned my children."

Jiho had to work hard not to cry. Not to rage at his father. Not to beg him to return to them.

"I'm sorry that I've been such a terrible dad," his father continued. "I know I don't deserve forgiveness. But it feels so good to see you again, Jiho."

"That makes one of us," Jiho retorted.

He stomped away, not knowing where to go. He didn't want to see his friends or Koko, and he definitely didn't want to see any namushin.

Even though Jiho was upset about seeing his father, he couldn't help but be amazed with the beauty of Mir. The old dragon world was the most spectacular place he'd ever seen. He felt a deep sadness to realize there were no more dragons in his world, and he found himself wishing he could see one in real life just once.

He wandered aimlessly through the old structures of Mir and came upon a familiar face in what was once a small courtyard of a beautiful marble building.

"Sister Yoon! Is that really you?" Jiho asked in surprise.

"Well, well, little Jiho Park. Nice to finally see you here in the Nackwon," old lady monk Yoon replied.

"Last I saw, you were in Hanoe village," Jiho exclaimed in surprise. "How in the world did you come to be in Nackwon, especially up here in Mir? I thought people who came here never left!"

"It's not that people can't leave, it's that they don't want to," the monk replied. "Just look at this place. You won't find anything like this in the world."

Jiho agreed. Beyond the small courtyard he could see the outer reaches of Mir and the layers of clouds floating below it. If not for his family, Jiho could see himself staying for a long time.

"So why do you leave?" Jiho asked.

"It's my job to roam the human world and bring back news to the Nackwon council," she answered.

"You're a spy?"

The monk laughed. "I guess you could say that. But I like to call myself a keeper of the peace."

She leaned forward to peer into Jiho's face. "I take it you saw your father?"

Jiho nodded.

"And judging by that sour expression, it didn't go too well."

"Just because he had a mission doesn't excuse him from deserting us," Jiho said bitterly. "He should have explained why he was leaving. We deserved that much at least."

"Completely agree with you," Sister Yoon said. "Your father is a very stubborn, stoic person who doesn't know how to express himself. Stupid pride. You need to learn to be a better human than your dad."

Jiho didn't know if he should be offended or not. But the monk continued on.

"It's good you are here. We will need all our strongest fighters in the days to come," the monk said.

"I'm not a fighter, and I'm definitely not strong."

The monk shot him a measuring look. "You still doubt yourself. You are a Park. Your family has been rangers of the Kidahara for centuries. Your blood is your strongest asset."

"What does being a Park have to do with anything?"

"You don't know who you really are," she said. "But you will learn soon enough."

Too tired to argue, Jiho just shook his head. Like the princess, he was suddenly overcome with exhaustion. "I just want to sleep," Jiho said.

The monk nodded sympathetically. "Follow the namushin. They will find you a place to rest."

CHAPTER 14

JIHO OPENED HIS eyes to the sight of a gorgeous sunrise. The namushin had taken him to his own small tree house. It was a one-roomed round structure with a comfortable hammock and sitting area to lounge in and its very own private bathroom. Jiho was curious about the plumbing. If it was magical, would it not work for him? He was both surprised and relieved to see that Nackwon relied on copper piping, like the rest of the world. He loved everything about this little house with its glorious views and cozy interior. It was the nicest home he'd ever stayed in. And yet, he suddenly found himself missing his family. He couldn't help but think about how much his sisters would adore the tree house too.

A knock on the door and the rustling voices of the

namushin reminded him that he was to meet Koko after breakfast. He followed his little namushin guide all the way down to the Kidasan Shijang. Back to old Granny's noodle shop, where the others had already begun eating without him.

"Thanks for waiting," he groused at them good-naturedly.

"This food is too good to wait," Shane said.

"Have you seen the princess?" Jiho asked.

Before they could answer, Koko walked into the room and sat next to Jiho. She seemed tired and down.

"Morning, Princess!" everyone called out.

Koko responded with a nod and a half smile but still didn't say a word.

After an awkward silence, Granny appeared with bowls of noodles for Jiho and the princess.

"Hey, Jiho," Frankie said around a mouthful of noodles. "So I hear your dad is like the top guy here."

Jiho shrugged, unhappy to think about his father again.

"Yeah, I heard your family has been rangers and experts of the Kidahara for centuries," Frankie continued. "That's so cool! So when do you officially become a ranger? Or are you one already?"

"I have no interest in being a ranger," Jiho said sharply. "Rangers have to survey the Kidahara constantly and are away from home for months at a time. And they're never around when you need them!"

Everyone was quiet.

Calvin cleared his throat. "Well, I've been meaning to ask why there isn't a Joson group on the training grounds."

"That's because the Joson are already integrated into the Nackwon army," Koko said. "They are magical, just like Nackwon folks."

The others nodded in understanding.

"Listen, Jiho," Calvin said. "We've all decided that we are going to stay here and train with our countrymen. Are you cool with that?"

"No, I'm quite warm," Jiho replied in some confusion.

Shane snickered. "What Calvin meant was are you good with our decision."

"Ah!" Jiho blushed.

"If that is what you wish, then I support it completely," Jiho replied.

"Thanks, Jiho," Calvin said. "Shane and I would love it if you joined the Bellprix and trained with us."

"Nah, you should join the Orions with me," Frankie said. "We'll be the best trainers."

"Don't be ridiculous. Everyone knows Urcian soldiers are better than all the rest. We excel at hand-to-hand combat, and Orion soldiers are useless without their weapons," Tess cut in, Jay nodding emphatically.

Jiho was touched by his friends' words. But before he could respond, Koko interrupted. "Actually, Jiho is going to have to train with me," she said. "That is what the namushin say."

"Me?" Jiho asked in surprise. "Why me?"

Koko shrugged and played apathetically with her noodles.

"What's up with her?" Frankie asked.

Tess and Jay hushed him.

Leaning closer to Jiho, Calvin whispered, "You okay with this? Because if not, you can stay with us. We're your friends. We've got your back." Shane, who had listened, nodded in agreement.

Jiho could feel an unusual warmth in his chest. He realized how happy he was to be a part of this group. For the first time in his life, he felt close to people other than his family. It was a strange but wonderful sensation that he cherished.

"It'll be fine," he said. "But I'm proud to call you my friends."

"Always." Calvin and Shane shook hands with Jiho as the others chimed in.

"Us too!" Tess and Jay shouted.

"Friends forever!" Frankie raised his glass, and everyone toasted in agreement.

Their good spirits seemed to make Koko more depressed. She rose to her feet abruptly and walked out.

"Well, that's rude," Frankie said in a huff.

Tess and Jay both shook their heads at him.

"Give her a break, Frankie," Tess said. "Her world has just been turned completely upside down. She's allowed to be upset."

Jay gave a wistful sigh. "Still, I would love to be a dragon."

As the friends left the noodle shop, they caught sight of Ranger Park and a small delegation of namushin waiting patiently for them outside. Koko stood a short distance away.

Jiho didn't acknowledge his father, but everyone else greeted him happily.

"Hey, Ranger Park!" Calvin said. "Were you waiting for us?"

Ranger Park nodded. "I'm here to take Jiho and the princess to Master Remauld's castle."

Jiho was surprised but refused to ask his father why he was going also. Instead, he turned to talk to his friends. Frankie was staring at Ranger Park's staff with curiosity.

"Excuse me, Ranger Park, but can I see your staff?" Frankie asked. "It looks extremely old."

Ranger Park drew back the staff from Frankie's outstretched hands. "I'm sorry, but this staff must never be touched by an outsider. Only Parks are allowed to handle it."

He stuck it in the band that was slung over his back.

Frankie looked disappointed, making Jiho irritated for some reason.

"Don't worry, Frankie. It's no big deal. Just an old wooden stick that doesn't do anything," Jiho said.

After saying goodbye to his friends, Jiho followed Koko, his father, and the namushin. They headed down a tunnel and entered a small loading dock with large benches attached to the floor and ceiling. Jiho squeezed onto the seat next to Koko, and his father and the bench moved into a narrow tunnel where winds whisked them through to an entirely new area of the Nackwon.

"So this tunnel travel isn't magic, huh?" Jiho asked.

"No, it's based on aerodynamics," Koko said. "But I have no idea how it works."

Jiho didn't know either, but he enjoyed the ride.

"Where are we going now?" he asked.

"To the wizard's guild," his father answered. "It is located on the farthest southern tip of Joson."

The tunnel ended at a pathway that led up to the outside world. Jiho could smell the tangy salt air and hear the cawing of seagulls.

"We're at the beach!"

He could see white sand and a vast deep blue ocean. But before they could step out of the cave, his father stopped them.

"I'll leave you both here for now," Ranger Park said. "I will be back in time to take you home at the end of your lesson."

The ride in the tunnel had restored some of Koko's good spirits, and she hugged the ranger goodbye. Jiho went ahead and stepped onto warm sand. In the distance, he could see tall, rocky formations rising up to a cliff with a castle perched on top. It looked completely different from the one in the dragon's realm. This was an old, dark-looking castle. Slightly sinister, even against the fluffy clouds that filled the bright blue skies.

"I think that's where we're supposed to go, Princess," Jiho said.

Koko looked peeved. "Well, if we can't use magic, how are we supposed to get up there?"

The namushin murmured, and then the little creatures jumped onto clouds that formed off the ocean waves and floated up into the sky.

"Oh, how amazing! We're going to cloud travel!"

Koko spun around, looking for a large-enough cloud. When she spotted one coming off a wave, she splashed toward it and jumped on with a big bounce. The cloud immediately began to rise up.

"Hurry up, Jiho!"

Jiho stood blinking his eyes for a moment before he glared at a nearby cloud that seemed to be floating close to him.

"I told you magic doesn't work on me."

"This isn't really magic, it's more like hybrid science. Cloud physics," Koko yelled back. "The rising air keeps you on the enhanced cloud as long as it's moving."

"Enhanced with what?"

He couldn't hear her response, as Koko had drifted too far from him. Skeptical, Jiho eyed the cloud. But when it began to float away, he took a deep breath and jumped on. To his amazement, the cloud not only held his weight, but it was surprisingly firm.

The cloud immediately followed Koko's in a direct trajectory to the castle, catching up rapidly.

"How is this not magic?" he said to himself. Suddenly, he noted that his butt was sinking through the cloud.

"Princess! I'm falling through!"

Koko turned around to stare down at him from her higher cloud height.

"Quick! Stop sitting all scrunched up and lie down, spread-eagle, before you fall out!"

Jiho scrambled to throw open his arms, but his butt had already sunk halfway through and he was sinking rapidly.

He heard Koko giggling above and knew he looked ridiculous. He scowled at her and was about to yell again when his lower torso fell completely through the cloud.

Trying not to panic, Jiho peeked to see how far up he was. The cloud was as high as the cliffs but still only halfway to the safety of the castle grounds. He looked out and saw he was almost over some dangerous-looking rocks that peppered the shoreline, right before the cliffs. Jiho swung his legs up into the cloud, but then he fell in to his armpits. He was now dangling half in and half out of the cloud.

"Princess, I'm falling!" he screamed. "I can't hold on anymore!"

Desperate, he grabbed at the cloud puffs, only to have them dissipate within his fingers. He was now at chin level, with his legs kicking into the air currents. Before he could scream again, his head sank completely into the cloud and through it. His legs kicked frantically as he fell through the air and landed with a thud onto the back of a vibrant fire-colored phoenix.

Jiho grabbed on to its feathers as it soared above Koko, who stared up at them in astonishment and excitement. The phoenix flew straight to the castle grounds and landed gently, allowing Jiho to slide down its beautiful tail feathers.

Koko and the namushin finally arrived and jumped down to greet the phoenix, who bowed its head in return. Its golden eyes blinked solemnly before it soared into the sky once again.

"Cloud physics, what dog poop!" Jiho muttered. He rounded on Koko. "Those clouds were enhanced by magic. I could've died!"

"It was only a little magic, and don't worry, the namushin and I wouldn't have let you die. We would've saved you!"

"How? You can't use magic on me," Jiho said.

Koko opened her mouth to respond and then closed it sheepishly. "I'm sorry. I keep forgetting. But the namushin told me you would be safe."

"How would they know?"

"Because they knew I sent Seraphina to catch you," Master Remauld said. "And just in time! Another minute and you would have been . . . ahem. Welcome to Kirin Keep!"

Koko and Jiho were startled by his sudden appearance,

but the namushin bowed and began a murmuring conversation with him.

Master Remauld listened carefully. "Yes, I see what you mean," he responded to the little creatures. "He nullified one of my strongest magic spells in less than a minute. Amazing. He is more powerful than his father."

Jiho scratched his head in consternation. "I'm sorry about that, sir. I didn't mean to do it. I just can't help myself."

"Hmmmm," Remauld murmured. "Very intriguing. I think it will be enlightening studying you, Jiho Park."

Jiho was confused. "You're going to study me? Why?"

"Because I find anomalies fascinating," Remauld said. "Now follow me."

The wizard led them into a large, spectacular courtyard with four trees in the separate corners, each representing a season. One cherry blossom tree was in full springtime bloom, with small pale pink petals blanketing the grass. The second tree was green and leafy and summery. The third tree was bathed in the glorious colors of autumn and falling leaves. The last one was barren and frozen, the only adornment were small icicles that hung from its branches. In the center of the courtyard was a colorful paved design, and Jiho stepped back to take in the large artwork. It was a dragon.

"That is the great dragon, Kirin, whom this keep is named after," Remauld said. "He was the strongest and wisest of the dragons. His great-great granddaughter, Nanami, was the most like him and a dear friend of mine. I miss her very much."

Jiho did a double take. The wizard didn't look any older than sixty.

"I'm seven hundred and ninety-eight years old," Remauld said with an amused smile. "And I'm not even the oldest of my kind."

Remauld then clapped his hands and a curtain of white fog surrounded them in a large circle.

"Princess, now is the time to begin to tap into your dragon magic. But in order to do so, you must awaken it from within."

"Dragon magic? How do I do that?"

"Only you know that answer," Remauld said. "But I am here to help you." He waved his hand and images of many dragons played on the white fog curtain. "Miran, Geroff, Celestine, and Nanami, the great dragon leaders and your ancestors."

Jiho and Koko stared at the moving images in awe. Miran was a white dragon with a golden mane, Geroff and Celestine were both blue dragons, and Nanami was a magnificent black dragon. The images shifted between their dragon forms and their human forms.

"I am eager to see your dragon, Princess," Remauld said.

Jiho's eyes widened. "Oh, wow! How cool! I bet you'll be a gold dragon with a black mane."

Koko backed away. "M-my dragon?" she stuttered.

"Yes, we are going to teach you how to transform into your dragon form."

"I can't do that!" Koko shouted. "What if I can't shift back?"

The wizard cast Jiho an amused look. "That is why he is here."

"Oh." Koko looked at Jiho with misery. "That's right. You nullify magic."

"Um, okay. Glad to help," Jiho said in surprise.

But Koko wasn't paying attention. She looked terribly upset. "I thought this was my regular magic-training session. I didn't know you were going to make me transform. I'm not ready!"

"That is why we are training," Remauld replied.

Koko shook her head violently. "No, I don't want to do this!"

It was Remauld's turn to look surprised. Something that Jiho guessed didn't happen too often.

"But why? It is who you are. Who you're supposed to be."

"I don't want to be a dragon. I want to be a human."

Remauld looked saddened for a moment. "I yearn for the days when my dragon friends flew free in the great skies. The glory. The magnificence. I wish you both could have seen it. I miss them all so terribly."

His sad eyes became gentle as he gazed at the princess. "You are not human, Princess. You are a dragon taking human form, yes. But that doesn't make you human."

"But why was I like this as a baby?" Koko cried, tears rolling down her face.

"You bonded with the queen in your egg and shifted to human form," Remauld said. "Call it a dragon's instinct for survival. To take on the form most pleasing to its caregivers."

She was quiet for a long time. "You mean it was a trick? It was all a lie? This isn't me?"

She dropped to the floor and covered her face.

Remauld waved away the curtain of dragons, bringing Jiho and Koko back to the courtyard. He knelt gently in front of the princess.

"What is it, child, that frightens you?"

She shook her head and began to cry. Immediately, the namushin gathered around her to comfort her.

The wizard stood and gazed thoughtfully at Jiho. "Come, let us leave the princess to gather her composure." He shooed the namushin out, but when Jiho made to follow, he gestured for him to stay.

Jiho scratched his head and dug his hands into his pockets. Not knowing what to do, he sat cross-legged in front of the princess. After several long minutes, she lifted her head to meet Jiho's uncomfortable gaze.

"I'm scared," she said. "I don't want to do this."

"Why?" Jiho asked. "You're the only dragon in the entire world. Isn't it important to represent them again?"

"But what if I can't switch back? What if I remain a dragon forever?"

"Why does that thought frighten you?"

Koko looked up and glanced at Jiho. "I like being human."

"Maybe you'll like being a dragon also."

"What if I don't want to be a dragon?"

"Are you kidding me?" Jiho sputtered. "Who wouldn't want to be a dragon?"

"Lots of people," Koko answered. "The reason the dragons joined Luzee was because humans tried to exterminate them."

"Yeah, but they were dumb and didn't know any better."

"What makes you so sure it would be different this time?"

Jiho couldn't answer her question. He didn't know and he couldn't assure her that all would be fine.

"I would protect you, Princess. And I would stay by your side."

"And you would still like me?"

"I think I might like you better as a dragon," he teased. "You know, for a dragon princess, you sure do cry a lot. Didn't they say dragons don't cry?"

Koko nodded, wiping away her tears with the back of her hand. "Dragon's tears are the most powerful medicine in the world. They say they could heal anyone, even those who are dying. But it is almost impossible for a dragon to cry."

"Well, I don't think that'll be a problem for you."

Koko shrugged. "I am a very intense, emotional person," she said with a slight smile.

"You must be scary when you're mad," Jiho said.

Her smile faded. "I don't want to be scary. I don't want people fearing me."

"I didn't mean it that way. . . ."

But the princess shook her head and clamped her hands over her ears. "No, no, no. This is all wrong. How can I be a dragon?" she cried. "I thought at most I had a little bit of dragon's blood. And I was proud of it. But to be a real dragon? To be the last dragon? No! It can't be! I won't let it be! I don't want to be a dragon!"

Her eyes fierce and angry, Koko stormed out.

"Princess, come back!" Jiho yelled. "You have to train."

"Train for what? To become a dragon?" Koko yelled. "I'm not going to let anyone force me to do anything, Jiho Park! And you should understand that better than anyone."

Jiho ran after her but found himself staring down an empty corridor. Koko had disappeared. Jiho ran through the castle and outside, but the princess was nowhere to be found. Nor were any namushin.

"Not wanting to be a ranger and not wanting to be a dragon isn't the same," he muttered to himself. "Dragons are cool."

"To you they are," Remauld said.

Jiho jumped, as the wizard appeared out of nowhere.

"But the princess is scared," Remauld said. "What if I told you that you are not Joson at all but a full-blooded Orion?"

"I am not!" Jiho was offended at the suggestion.

The wizard smiled. "Orions and Joson are still human. Imagine finding out that you aren't even of the same species."

Jiho nodded in understanding, appreciating the wizard's explanation. He turned to ask a question that had been troubling him for a while.

"Master Remauld, why was there only one dragon egg? Shouldn't there have been others? How could dragons go extinct so easily?"

The wizard's expression turned sad. "The reason there were so few dragons in the world was because of how hard it was for them to breed. If we were lucky, we would see a dragon's egg once a year. But as time passed, there were many years where no young dragons were hatched at all."

"That is so sad," Jiho said.

"And that is why we must help the princess fulfill her destiny. Because the world needs dragons again."

Remauld vanished, and in his place was Seraphina, the phoenix, who preened and shook out her beautiful sunset wings.

"That is so rude," Jiho said peevishly as he petted the phoenix. "Bet he knew I had more questions and he didn't want to answer them."

Seraphina gave him a nudge and lowered her back. With a sigh, Jiho climbed on and held tight as the majestic creature soared into the sky.

CHAPTER 15

JIHO SEARCHED ALL over Mir until he finally found Koko in the dragon queen's castle.

"When I first came here, I thought I was only slightly related to her," Koko said. "Turns out I might actually be her kid."

She laughed bitterly. "I just can't get used to this."

Jiho started to speak, but Koko put her hand up to stop him.

"If you're going to tell me again how much you wish you were a dragon, I shall scream."

He quickly clamped his mouth shut again.

He looked around the spacious room and noted the rich upholstery of the seating area and the many beautiful vases, jewelry boxes, and artwork decorating the entire space.

Paintings with bold, vibrant colors and tapestries with delicate stitchwork framed the many walls, while statues of all sorts of magic folk were showcased. It struck him that everything was at his eye level. The chair he was sitting in was oversize but comfortable. He would not have pictured a dragon queen's private rooms to feel so human.

"Princess, if the dragon queen only used her human form around other humans, then why are her chambers here so small and humanlike?"

The princess sat up and looked around Nanami's chambers. "These were her private rooms," she said slowly. "For when she wanted to be alone and rest."

"She must have liked being in her human form," Jiho said.

"The namushin have been teaching me dragon history, and I learned that dragons could shape-shift to any form they wanted. But that they all had one that was their favorite. All royal dragons preferred their human form over all others, because they felt the human brain was closest to that of a dragon's."

"Well, that's pretty interesting!" Jiho exclaimed. He peered at Koko's face and noted that she looked deep in thought. "Why do you think that is, Princess?"

"Probably because a dragon's brain is quite complex and so is a human's," Koko replied absentmindedly. "There was a story about a dragon whose favorite form was an ogre's. But apparently changing into an ogre affected his dragon's brain. Made him duller and he became more and more ogre-like until one day he left Mir and never came back. The namushin claim that he lived his life from then on out as an ogre."

"So he became too dumb to be a dragon anymore?" Jiho laughed. "Why in the world did he decide to shape-shift into an ogre in the first place? They're dumb, hideous-looking, and they smell foul."

"Especially since dragons hate being dirty!" Koko said. "They're very fastidious."

Jiho looked Koko up and down, taking note of her grass-stained clothing and wild, unbrushed mop of hair.

"Are you sure you're a dragon?"

Koko began pelting Jiho with pillows, as the room echoed with their laughter.

As Koko's mood lifted, the namushin appeared and whispered their message to her.

Koko sighed. "Okay, I'm ready to go back."

Back at Kirin Keep, Wizard Remauld smiled at their return.

"Let us begin the training."

Remauld pulled the curtain of fog around them again.

"Dragon magic is the most powerful magic of all," Remauld said. "It doesn't rely on spells or thoughts. It simply is."

"I don't understand what that means," Koko said.

"You just have to be who you are," Remauld replied.

"Release the magic from deep within you. The one that comes from your soul."

Jiho sat on a bench and watched as the wizard tutored the dragon princess. The namushin hopped onto the bench and made themselves comfortable on his lap and his shoulder. Jiho smiled as he heard their little purrs of contentment.

After several hours of practicing, Koko still couldn't manifest any dragon magic. Frustrated, she had a temper tantrum and released an explosion of electrical sparks. The wizard blocked them with a wave of his hand, and the namushin scrambled away. But several hit Jiho and let off a huge cloud of sparks.

"I'm so sorry, Jiho!" Koko cried. "Are you okay?"

Jiho coughed and waved away the smoke. "I told you, magic doesn't work on me," he said. "I'm immune."

Koko was intrigued. "But when I zap your dad, he gets stunned for a little bit. You aren't affected at all?"

Jiho scratched his head. "I don't know, it seems to be stronger for me and my sisters. My dad said that before I was born they could at least have basic magic spells around the house. But when my sisters and I are all together, we cancel all magic around us by our mere presence."

"Can you do that yourself?"

Jiho shook his head. "But if you direct any magic toward me, it won't work."

Koko turned her finger blue and touched Jiho with it.

Immediately her finger turned normal again, with only a ring of blue left at the bottom of her finger.

"Wow, you really do cancel out all magic. That's quite a power to have," Koko said.

"It's not a power," Jiho said. "I have no magic."

"No, Jiho, it's actually the deepest kind of magic," Remauld said, approaching them. "It's the most powerful. It's immunity."

He pointed his finger at a floating leaf and transformed it into a large green frog and let it leap into Jiho's face. Jiho shrieked and caught the frog with his hands, and it immediately turned back into a leaf.

"Your father said that Parks have been rangers of the Kidahara for centuries," Koko said. "I bet this was an important power to have as they patrolled the Kidahara."

Jiho shrugged. "I never thought much about it. But I guess it helped keep them from being killed every day."

"What else can you do?" Koko asked.

Jiho shook his head. "I told you I can't do magic. I can't do anything."

Koko looked at him dubiously. "Your father can find anything he wants in the forest," she said. "He definitely has magic. Therefore you must also. Maybe you've never tried."

"If I am immune to magic, how can I make magic?"

"I know it sounds strange, but I'm sure you're magical,

Jiho," Koko said. "I can feel it. Isn't that right, Master Remauld?"

The wizard gazed thoughtfully at Jiho.

"She's right," Remauld said. "You are here not only to help train the princess but also for me to try to discern the true level of your magical ability, beyond your immunity."

Jiho scoffed at that. "I told you, I don't have any."

Remauld nearly smiled.

"Actually you do," he said. "And you will need them in the coming war. I'm sure of it."

"How am I of any help?"

"In a war of magic, your talent could be the difference between victory and annihilation."

Jiho was intimidated by the wizard's words. He didn't know how he could be so important, and he was chilled by the idea of perilous war. He was finally beginning to realize that something dangerous was brewing.

Over the next couple of days, Jiho came to Koko's training. Although instead of cloud travel, the wizard made sure to have Seraphina waiting for him at the portal door. Jiho became very fond of the beautiful phoenix. Seraphina was gentle and affectionate and took Jiho for a long flight around Kirin Keep before dropping him off in the courtyard.

Koko became very envious. "Why can't I ride Seraphina?"

"Because Seraphina would not take kindly to letting a dragon ride her," Remauld responded.

"But why?"

"That is not the natural order of things. While you may be a dragon princess, Seraphina is queen of all birds."

"That's not fair," Koko groused.

"If you want to fly, Princess, then I suggest you transform into your dragon self and show Seraphina how a dragon does it."

"I'm trying!" Koko stuck her tongue out at the wizard and went back to learning transformation. The wizard told Koko to start by learning the magic of transforming other things before she could transform herself. She was a quick study and could already change butterflies into peacocks and cats into tigers. Now she was growing scales on fruit.

Jiho was learning how to converse with the namushin when he heard a loud angry shout. He looked up in amazement to see that Koko had managed to grow scales all over her body. The same golden scales he'd seen on baby Koko.

"I can't get them off!" Koko cried.

Jiho ran over and grabbed her arm, and they watched as the scales quickly changed back to skin.

"Thanks, Jiho," she said.

"You're getting closer!"

Koko nodded. "I'm still scared."

"I'm not," Jiho said. "You're gonna be beautiful."

CHAPTER 16

JIHO AND KOKO's daily routine was to head to Granny's for lunch. Sometimes one or more of the Omni crew would join them, and they would always have a fun meal together. But most days, Jiho would eat alone with the princess, and they would spend time talking about their families. It was then that he found himself missing his uncle and aunt and sisters the most.

"Why don't you talk to your dad?" Koko asked. "Do you blame me for your dad deserting you?"

"No, of course not," Jiho exclaimed. "What he did had nothing to do with you!"

"That's not true. He left you to take care of me at the namushin's request. So it's my fault."

"Koko, my dad deserted us long before he went to help you."

The princess was silent, and then she smiled. "You called me Koko."

Jiho was aghast. "I'm sorry, Princess, I mean, Your Highness."

She shushed him. "I like it when you call me Koko. It makes me feel like your friend. You're my friend, aren't you?"

"Yes, I'm your friend," Jiho said.

Koko clapped her hands in delight. "I've never had a friend who was my age before."

She furrowed her eyebrows as she thought some more. "Come to think of it, I've never had a human friend either."

Before she could continue, a messenger arrived. "Princess, there is a Joson person at the gates making a ruckus and calling for you."

"For me?"

"Yes, it's a young girl, and she says she has an important message for you from your parents. But she won't give it to anyone but you."

At his words, Koko flew out of the shop, Jiho close at her heels. They raced through the tunnels and headed to the Nackwon portal gates, when Jiho's father stopped them.

"Princess, I must advise you not to go out," he said. "We don't know who she is or what she wants."

"But it's a message from my parents," Koko said. "I have to know."

"Then we will come with you."

Ranger Park stepped out first with several of the princess's guards before he allowed Koko and Jiho to join them. When they did, Jiho recognized the young messenger immediately.

"Hey, that's the bandit who stole my bag!"

Micah ignored him and focused all her attention on the princess.

"Princess Koko, I come from Joson and have terrible news for you," Micah said.

Ranger Park put up a hand to stop her from continuing. "First, who are you, and how did you know where the princess was?"

"My name is Micah Valon. I am the leader of the Botan clan," she said. "We are traders by profession and bandits who steal from the rich and give to those in need. But ever since Prince Roku came to Joson, he has filled the country with Orion soldiers and has made life extremely difficult for my clan. That is how I ran into the foreigners. We were desperate and stole from them."

"And threatened to kill us!" Jiho interrupted.

The bandit leader bowed her head. "My apologies. It was to keep my clan from starving. But that is when I saw the princess. I recognized her immediately. So I went to Jinju to tell the queen that the lost princess was safe and hopefully gather the reward money. That is when I found out that Prince Roku had staged a coup and is now proclaiming himself the king of Joson."

"But what about my parents?" Koko asked in fright.

"He arrested them and threw them in the dungeon," Micah said. "They are all right, but I don't know for how long. The conditions are terrible down there, and your mother is weak. I was able to see her, and she gave me this to give to you."

Micah pulled out the butterfly comb and held it in the light where it sparkled in the sunlight.

"My favorite comb!"

Koko reached out to grab it, but Ranger Park stopped her. "Let me examine it first, Princess."

He took the comb from Micah and covered it between his hands for a long moment. Examining the comb carefully, he walked over to Jiho.

"Here, son," he said. "Let's make doubly sure there is no magic on it before you give it to the princess."

Nodding, Jiho held the comb. He felt nothing. No buzz or tingle that usually marked a magical item.

"It's clean," he said, and handed it to Koko.

Tears had begun to leak from Koko's eyes as soon as she saw her comb. But now, she couldn't hold back. "Mama, Papa! I need to save them!"

"I don't think that is a good idea," Ranger Park said. "It's most likely a trap. As long as you are alive, Prince Roku's claim to the throne is illegitimate. You must not return."

"I don't care! I have to save my parents!"

"I could guide you into the city and the palace without

Roku knowing," Micah said. "I could take you to them."

"You can? We could rescue my parents?"

"No, that is impossible," Ranger Park said. "It's too dangerous."

"Nothing is impossible," Micah said.

"Thank you for your message," Ranger Park said. "I'll make sure you are rewarded for your time."

He had the soldiers escort Micah out, but as she left, she twisted around and shouted to Koko one last time. "Just remember, the Botan clan can help you, Princess."

After the soldiers escorted her far from the Nackwon boundary, Micah pulled out the moonstone that she always carried with her everywhere. Micah could now handle it without any pain. It glowed stronger than ever, but the nightmares that had plagued her had stopped. Micah knew it was because of Samena, the mysterious fairy she'd pledged her loyalty to. Holding the moonstone to her chest, Micah whispered Samena's name.

Soon the beautiful fairy appeared before her again.

"Have you seen the princess?"

"Yes, I spoke to her," Micah replied.

"Where was she, and who was she with?" Samena asked.

Micah gave the fairy a detailed rundown of the meeting with the princess.

"You should have forced her to come with you." Samena's voice was icy cold.

"Don't worry, she will come," Micah replied. "I'm sure of it."

"She'd better," Samena retorted. "The next step is to reunite the moonstones."

"But do you know where the others are?" Micah asked.

A thin smile crossed Samena's face. "Oh, yes, I know. I've always known."

CHAPTER 17

THE NEXT NIGHT, Jiho sat hidden in the shadows of the tree outside the Nackwon portal gate. He hadn't waited long when he saw a familiar figure sneaking out of the tree.

"So how'd you get past my father?" Jiho asked.

Koko jumped and smiled in relief to see Jiho. "Oh, it's just you. I was wondering where you went."

"So you could give me a special hot drink to sleep also?"

"You saw that? Don't worry; it was just valerian root. He'll be a bit groggy in the morning, but it won't hurt him."

"You can't go alone," he said. "And how can you trust that girl? She's a thief."

"She's an honorable thief," Koko said. "And I need to help my parents."

"Do you have any idea how you plan on freeing them?"

"I will magic them out," Koko said.

Jiho shook his head skeptically. "I don't know that your magic is that strong."

"That's why we're going to find the Botan clan," Koko said. "I'm sure they will help us."

"More like they'll ransom us."

"Please don't stop me," Koko begged. "The namushin won't let me go to help them, but they're my parents. The only ones I have, and I've missed them so much. I left them once—I'm not going to desert them again."

"I can't believe you made it this far without a namushin ratting you out!"

Koko looked guilty. "I may have placed a little spell on them."

"On all of them?"

"Well, the trick is to bespell all the trees in the area to sleep, and any namushin in range will fall asleep too."

"Okay, maybe your magic *is* strong enough!"

"So does that mean you won't stop me?"

Jiho sighed. "Good thing I packed a bag with food and supplies, as I see you've left with a small bag of . . . just what, may I ask, is in that small purse?"

With an irritated huff, Koko opened her purse and pulled out a large flask and a sleeping bag. "I bet you didn't pack any water or a sleeping bag, did you? Or what about extra shoes or boots and clean socks?"

Jiho's mouth dropped open. "What kind of wacky magical bag is that?"

"It's a space-saver bag," Koko said. "I took it from Kirin Keep when Master Remauld wasn't looking. Just watch."

She put the purse on the ground and tapped it twice while chanting, "Enlarge!" The purse transformed into a large suitcase. Koko then tapped it once and said, "Reduce."

"Now who's making fun of my little purse?"

Koko ended by sticking out her tongue.

"Just how long do you think we're going to be gone?" Jiho asked.

"I don't know," Koko said. "But better to be prepared for anything."

"Hm, I wonder what would happen if I touched it?" Jiho started to reach for the bag.

"Don't you dare!" Turning up her nose, Koko began to march away.

"So do you know where we're going?" Jiho asked.

"I'm using a finder spell," Koko said, holding up a small round compass. "It will point us to the closest Botan clan member, which should be Micah."

Jiho peered over to look at the compass, and immediately the arrow went spinning. Koko pushed him away.

"Not so close! You're messing it up!"

Jiho stopped in a huff. "Well, I'll just go back then if I'm not wanted. . . ."

With a gasp, Koko grabbed him by the arm. "No, please. I'm sorry. I definitely want you with me," she said with a conciliatory smile. "We'll just figure out how close we can be and still have my spells work, okay?"

Jiho nodded.

"Do you want me to put your bag in my space-saver?" Koko asked.

"No, I'm good," Jiho replied. He shifted the heavy bag on his back. "I'd like to keep it, just in case we get split up or you lose your bag."

"I'm not going to lose my bag, silly!" Koko retorted.

They bickered amicably as they walked through the forest. After a while, Koko stopped talking and held her finger to her lips. "We're out of namushin land now," she said. "We don't want to attract anything dangerous if we don't have to."

Jiho agreed fervently, remembering the nightwalker and the other frightening creatures of the Kidahara. Being with Koko had lulled him into a false sense of security. He had to remember where he was and to always respect the Kidahara.

It wasn't until midday that they finally found the bandits. Or to be more accurate, the bandits found them. They seemed to converge on them from thin air. Three Botan clan warriors with black headbands adorned with their signature white peony insignia. All of them holding their double swords in attack mode.

Once again Jiho experienced the unpleasant sensation of being surrounded by a group of hostiles holding very sharp, scary knives.

"We're looking for Micah Valon," Koko said.

"I'm here, Princess," Micah said, appearing from behind a tree. "You've come just in time. Another day and we would have been gone."

"You said you could get us into the city and the palace without being detected," Koko said. "I need to see my parents. I need to get them out of there."

"Yes, of course, Your Highness. We can help you."

Koko smiled in relief. "I'm so glad you found me," she said. "Thank you so much. I won't ever forget this."

"Of course," Micah said smoothly. "It would be wonderful if Your Highness would remember the Botan clan and reward us in the near future."

"You will be rewarded handsomely!"

Jiho narrowed his eyes as he stared at the bandit girl. For a split second, he thought he'd seen an expression of guilt flash on her face. But it was gone so quickly, he couldn't be sure. However, one thing he knew for certain. He didn't trust her.

As they walked, Koko began to pepper the clan members with questions about themselves and their way of life.

Although Jiho found most of them taciturn and silent, it was hard to remain cold in the face of Koko's bright chatter.

She magically fixed a hole in the bottom of one clan member's boot and found a lost lucky charm for another. And she listened in fascination as Mari explained the importance of all the magic roots found in the Kidahara.

"Look, Princess, over there! What do you see?" Mari asked. She pointed to a patch where long curly-headed ferns grew wild.

"Brackenhead fiddlers!"

Mari laughed. "Bracken fiddleheads. They're ferns and very delicious, but in large amounts it can make you very sick and even kill you."

"Or just give you really bad gas," Jiho said.

"Or give you really bad gas that kills you," Micah cut in.

"What? I've never heard of gas killing anyone," Jiho retorted.

"Oh yeah? Well, it killed my cousin Mung," Micah said. "He was this really big guy who just loved to eat them. In fact, he loved fiddleheads so much, he refused to ever go without them. His mom had to gather extra bushels of the stuff to dry for the winter to satisfy his constant craving. I remember when we would have family meals with him, no one could ever get any fiddleheads, because he'd always hog them for himself, leaving us with not even a single piece." Micah shook her head sadly. "One day I was determined to get some ferns for dinner, so I sat myself next to Mung, ready to grab some as soon as my aunt brought them out. When Mung saw what I was waiting to do, he grabbed the entire plate, licked his chopsticks, and stirred them into the ferns so that no one else would want to eat any."

Koko pulled a disgusted face while Jiho snorted with suppressed laughter.

"Then one day, Mung got a very bad stomachache coupled with a high fever. He suffered in agony for many days. Nothing relieved the pain. He couldn't eat or drink. He just rolled on his bed, moaning terribly. It wasn't until the fourth day that Mung rolled over and let out a tremendous fart. It was so loud that all the neighbors thought it was thunder and wondered if a storm was approaching."

Koko stared in horrified fascination at Micah as Jiho pressed his hands to his mouth, trying desperately not to howl with laughter.

"After farting, my cousin immediately declared that he was starving and demanded to be served a big meal. His mom rushed to prepare his favorite dinner of rice, fish, and fiddleheads. Well, Mung took one bite of the ferns with his rice, farted again, and yelled 'I'm dying!' before expiring on the spot." Micah ended her story with a somber shake of her head. "It was the fiddleheads that killed him."

"How can you possibly know what it was he died from?" Koko asked.

"Oh, we're absolutely positive," Micah said. "His fart was so powerful, it knocked out the wall behind him. Left a big hole. Holding that much gas in your body acts like a poison, you know."

A mad giggle escaped Jiho.

Koko rolled her eyes. "I don't know what's so funny about body functions," she said.

All the clan members laughed.

Koko ignored them all and asked Micah, "Did your cousin really die from passing gas?"

"Well, if it wasn't the fart that killed him, it was the smell that did him in!" Micah replied. "The stench was so powerful that months after he died, if you passed too close to his house, it would knock you out. It burned all my nose hairs off. I still can't smell things out of my left nostril."

Koko looked so horrified and disgusted that Jiho completely lost it and laughed until tears leaked from his eyes.

"Don't worry, Princess," Mari said. "Micah's cousin Mung is still alive and eating fiddleheads as we speak."

Koko glared at Jiho, who was still laughing hard. "It's not that funny," she grumped and then marched ahead.

It took them two days of walking to reach the outskirts of the forest where Micah had set up a rendezvous with her clan members. There they found horses and a brightly colored closed wagon, plus several new Botan clan members.

"Today is market day," Micah said. "We'll go to the town

square to sell our products, and from there we'll get to the palace."

Micah went into the wagon and came back with Botan clan uniforms.

"Put these on," she said. "You are now part of our clan."

Koko snatched up the clothing and went toward the wagon when Micah stopped her. "Sorry, Princess, you'll have to change in the forest. This wagon is off-limits. It is packed with all our goods."

Several minutes later, Koko returned dressed in the black and white colors of the Botan clan. Micah looked her over critically.

"Is there any way you can change your hair color? It's too distinctive," she said. "We need something not so memorable."

With an excited nod Koko pointed at her hair and changed it to a dull mousy brown.

At that moment, Jiho came up to them and Micah gestured to him. "Change him also."

"Oh, I can't change his hair," Koko said. "He's got—"

"A phobia against changing my hair color," Jiho said. He gave Koko a stern glare. He didn't want anyone to know about his ability. "Besides, nobody knows me, so I don't have to change anything."

Micah shrugged. "Suit yourself. Let's hit the road."

The road to Jinju was surprisingly empty of travelers.

"Strange," Koko remarked. "I wonder where all the

people are. Usually the roads are packed on market day."

It was strange, Jiho thought. Market days were always the busiest days for any town. This didn't seem right.

"Princess," Jiho whispered. "I have a bad feeling about this. We should leave now."

Shaking her head, Koko refused to listen to him. "I'm going, Jiho, whether you come or not."

Frustrated by her stubbornness, Jiho vowed to be vigilant.

Chapter 18

In town, the streets were more crowded, but subdued. There was a tenseness, a nervousness, like people were waiting for something bad to happen. And the Botan clan members had grown very serious. No smiles, no jokes. They all knew they were facing danger, but Jiho was more certain than ever that his suspicions were correct. They were walking into a trap. Jiho could feel it in his gut. But how would he save the princess? How could he tell her that this clan that she had grown to like and laugh with were about to betray her?

He needed to talk to her. But he couldn't get Koko alone. Micah kept close to her side, and Mari or another clan member would subtly step in front of Jiho, keeping him away. Once in the marketplace, the clan members parked the wagon at the least busiest corner. Jiho and Koko were given the task of setting up the stalls while the others emptied the wagon and began hawking their wares.

Jiho's nerves were taut. There was no one else loudly advertising their wares. Only the Botan clan. As if they were letting others besides the shoppers know that they were there. He could see that Koko was unaware of anything except the palace looming in the distance.

"Princess, we have to get away," Jiho whispered. "This is a setup. They've sold us out."

"I don't believe it," Koko said. "They wouldn't do that to us. They are good people."

But before he could speak, loud shouting could be heard. From the other side of the marketplace, soldiers were searching the stalls, taking people in for questioning.

"They're looking for contraband," Mari said. "But they also heard a rumor that the princess is here."

"Princess, Jiho, we have to hide you in the wagon!" Micah whispered.

Jiho balked. This was the trap.

Micah looked at him. "I can't believe you still don't trust me," she said. She handed him a key. "This is the key to the wagon. Lock yourself in and stay quiet."

She pushed them over to the wagon. The door was open, and Koko made to enter but Jiho hung back.

"Your lack of trust is going to cost the princess her life," Micah said sharply. "They're going to be here any minute, and you don't have any papers."

"Jiho, please," Koko begged.

Unsure and nervous, Jiho followed Koko into the dark wagon. Micah closed the door behind them. Inside it was pitch-black.

"There's something really strange about this," Jiho said. "I don't like it. And how am I supposed to lock the door when I can't see anything!"

"This wagon is strange," Koko said. "It is making me feel sick."

"Oh no," Jiho said.

Just then they heard the click of a lock and the wagon lurched forward. They both fell to the ground. Jiho saw the walls of the wagon fall off and light stream in from the narrow bars of what was now their moving prison cell. Rage filled Jiho when he saw Orion soldiers leading their wagon away, and the traitorous Botan clan members riding alongside.

"I knew we shouldn't have trusted you!" Jiho shouted at Micah.

Once again, Jiho thought he saw a flicker of guilt before it was gone. Micah gave a slight smile and bowed. "You should have listened to your instincts. That was a foolish mistake on your part."

"Jiho," Koko called. "I don't feel good. Something is burning me."

She was lying down on the floor, and steam rose from where her bare skin was touching the iron. Jiho hurried to pick her up and hold her in his lap.

Iron was deadly to magical creatures.

"Princess, the entire floor is iron. You have to try to keep your feet up," Jiho whispered.

Koko nodded weakly. Her hair color had turned back to normal, and she was able to open her eyes. But she started shivering. "Thank you for holding me. It's not as bad now."

But Jiho could see that being surrounded by bars of iron was sickening her. He carefully removed his bag from his back and reached in for the blanket he'd packed for the trip. It was a soft, warm, moss-green blanket that he'd taken from his tree house. The image of his little home in the Nackwon flitted through his mind and made him wish he'd never left. Shaking off the useless thought, Jiho wrapped the blanket snugly around the princess, careful to make sure no part of her was touching the iron walls or floor.

"Don't worry, Princess, I'll take care of you."

The soldiers drove them through the heart of the city, where quiet, somber-faced citizens stood by and watched. Jiho could hear some people whispering the princess's name while others openly wept. He realized this was not a city that welcomed Roku's takeover.

"Jiho," Koko whispered. "I'm feeling a little better now."

"That's great," Jiho said in relief.

"I think as long as I'm touching you, your immunity negates my magic, which is what makes me sick from the iron," Koko replied. "Help me put the blanket on the floor so I can sit on it."

Grabbing the blanket, he spread it on the ground next to him. Koko slid onto it, crossed her legs, and leaned against Jiho's shoulder.

"As long as you are here, I can recharge my strength and use it to help us escape," Koko said. "But it is going to be a one-shot thing, because once I let you go, I won't have long before the iron affects me again. I was dumb before. I can't afford to make another mistake."

"Princess, you're not dumb for trusting people," Jiho said. "You're really smart and kind and generous and honest and everyone likes and respects you so much and . . . are you crying again?"

Koko nodded, sniffling against Jiho's shirt.

"And disgusting . . . ," Jiho continued.

She giggled, but it got caught into a hiccup. "Thanks for that," she said.

"What? Calling you disgusting? I have more insults for you if you want."

"No, thanks for being my friend," she said. "I've never had one before. A real friend."

Jiho was quiet for a moment. "Thanks for being mine too, Princess."

"Koko," she said.

"Koko," he replied. He put his arm around her shoulders and gave them a companionable squeeze. "I'm glad I came with you. Don't worry. Everything is going to work out."

Jiho stared at all the soldiers surrounding them and wasn't sure he believed his own words.

CHAPTER 19

THE WAGON ROLLED down the streets of Jinju, heading toward the palace. There was no warning when the attack came. One moment they were rolling slowly down the cobblestoned streets and the next they came to a crashing halt. Jiho and Koko stood up to get a better look at what was happening. Blocking the street was Master Remauld. With a snap of his fingers, he disarmed all the Orion soldiers. Rifles, guns, knives, and swords went flying behind him into a glowing magical space that disappeared once the last of the weapons flew in. At that moment, soldiers fell out of the sky and attacked the now weaponless Orions and Botan clan members.

"My soldiers!" Koko cried out. "They've come to rescue us!"

Jiho was shocked to see all his Omni Murtagh friends

suddenly fighting Orion soldiers. Even Frankie was there, enthusiastically punching several people in a row. And he even saw his father valiantly using his staff, bashing people left and right.

But before he could say anything, the wagon lurched off at a high speed. An Orion soldier had climbed aboard and was whipping the horses.

"Jiho, we have to get out of here now," Koko said.

"Are you sure you're strong enough?" Jiho asked.

"I think so," Koko answered. She squeezed Jiho's hand to reassure him.

"At the count of three, let go," she said. "One, two, three!"

Jiho released Koko's arm and scooted all the way back. Koko let out a blast of magic that blew down the walls and sent soldiers flying through the air. Jiho lurched to catch Koko as they fell off the wagon and hit the ground hard.

"Koko, we have to run," Jiho said.

She sat up and grabbed her head. "I'm so dizzy."

Before Jiho could urge her to go again, he saw a battalion of soldiers coming toward them.

"Halt or we'll shoot!"

The soldiers drew their weapons as they approached.

Jiho froze. "Koko, we need your magic—can you try it?" he whispered.

She stood determinedly and took a deep breath. Koko swirled her hands round and round, capturing magnetized air into a ball. Faster and faster it spun, sparks shooting out of it like fireworks.

"What are you waiting for? Shoot her!" someone screamed. The soldiers stopped, ready to fire.

Koko took a deep breath in and then shot her arms out hard, sending the ball of air exploding into the ground in front of the soldiers and scattering them all in a hundred directions.

"That was brilliant!" Jiho shouted. He turned back to catch Koko before she crumpled to the ground once more.

"Koko, what's the matter?"

She was breathing shallowly, and her complexion had turned deathly pale. "The iron must have affected me a lot more than I thought. I feel wiped out."

Jiho held her. "Come on, we have to get out of here."

Supporting her around the waist, Jiho looked for a way out of the city.

"Princess! Thank the heavens I've found you!"

They turned around to see Ranger Park arriving with Jiho's friends.

Relief flooded Jiho at the sight of his father. He was reminded of when he was little and the sense of safety that he always felt when he was around his dad. It was why his leaving had been so much harder for Jiho.

"There is no time to lose, we must get you out of the city!" Ranger Park said.

"My parents," Koko cried. She turned to stare at the

palace that was now a short distance away.

"The last thing they would want is for you to be imprisoned too," Ranger Park said. "We have to escape! Now."

The Omni Murtagh crew surrounded Koko and urged her along. Ranger Park took the lead, while Calvin and Shane positioned themselves in the back. They were all armed with heavy staffs similar to Ranger Park's. Jiho was happy to see his friends. Tess and Jay flanked Koko, holding their staffs protectively around her while Frankie patted Jiho on the back. "You should've told us what you were doing, Jiho," he said. "We would've come with you."

"You mean you would've stopped us," Jiho retorted.

"Yeah, that's what I really meant." Frankie smiled.

But his smile abruptly died when they found their way blocked. The Botan clan had found them. There in the front, by Micah's side, stood a fair-haired woman in a gray hooded cloak.

"I've seen her before," Jiho said. He had a flashback of the cloaked woman talking to Brock Murtagh back in Hanoe. Same gray cloak, same white hair.

"Who is she?" Frankie asked.

As if she heard their question, the woman answered.

"I am the fairy Samena," she said. "And I am in desperate need of Princess Koko's services. If the princess were to come with me, I would help free her parents from the dungeons."

Koko began to approach her, but Ranger Park held her back.

"Don't trust her, Princess," he said. "We don't know who she is or what she wants."

"I only want what we all want," the fairy said. "I want what is best for the Kidahara. Of course our opinions might differ on what that might be. But I'm sure I will be able to persuade you that my way is the right way."

"I don't think so," Ranger Park growled. He held his staff in front of him, readying himself for the fight. "You'll not take the princess from us."

The fairy fell silent, staring in fascination at the staff in his hands. Her eyes glittered malevolently.

"Jiho," Ranger Park whispered. "Take the princess and head for the east gate. Our forces are convening there. Tess and Jay will guide you."

The fairy finally spoke again.

"You also have something that I need," she said. "Something that used to be mine. And now I want it back."

"Come and get it," Ranger Park yelled.

The Botan clan stepped forward, and with a wave of her hands, Samena conjured up swords for them.

"Sticks and stones may break your bones, but knives will always kill you," Samena taunted. "Bring me the princess and that staff."

Micah bowed and with a loud cry, the Botan clan attacked.

"Go now!" Ranger Park shouted before smashing his staff on the head of an attacker.

Tess and Jay hustled Koko away, but Jiho stared at his father, suddenly afraid for his well-being. He seemed so alone and vulnerable in a way Jiho was not used to. He took a step toward his father when Tess called for him.

"Jiho! Get over here!" Tess ordered. "You help the princess, I'll lead, and Jay will cover us from the back."

Jiho nodded and grabbed hold of Koko, who was too weak to walk on her own. But his mind was still on his father. He wanted to go back and help him. Yet his responsibility was to Koko. His father would never forgive him if he abandoned her. And he would never forgive himself either. Koko needed him.

Resolute, Jiho followed Tess as they made their way to the east gate. They weaved their way through crowded streets, hiding from soldiers.

"We're almost there," Tess said.

"Watch out!" Jay shouted. Heavily armed Orion soldiers were patrolling the gate.

They stopped and pivoted into a side street, only to come face-to-face with the Botan clan.

Just then a large runaway wagon barreled into the Botan clan, sending them flying. Off jumped Ranger Park, Calvin, Shane, and Frankie.

Jiho was relieved to see all of them, but especially his father.

"This way," Ranger Park said. They could hear the shouting of the soldiers attracted by the noise. Weaving in and out of side streets, they bypassed the soldiers and came back to the east gate. This time only Micah and Samena stood blocking their way. The fairy somehow looked bigger than before, as if she'd magically enhanced her size.

"I'm afraid I can't let you go," Samena said. With a flick of her hands, fire shot out in a fantastic blaze.

Before the fire could reach them, Master Remauld appeared and formed a protective barrier of crystal magic. He sent a lightning bolt that crashed onto the spot where Samena was standing. Micah and the other soldiers were thrown back from the strike, but Samena had vanished. She reappeared only a second later, and her form seemed to flicker with anger. What happened next was a wild and furious battle between two powerful magical beings.

During the fury of battle, Remauld unleashed a magic strike that destroyed the city wall, to the far left of the fairy.

"Go, now!" he shouted. "I shall cover you."

Samena unleashed a rapid volley of fireballs, setting the entire area ablaze. From behind, an army of Orion soldiers appeared in attack formation.

"Koko, if you can do anything at all, this might be a good time to use your magic," Jiho whispered.

She nodded weakly and staggered away from him. She faced the army behind them and took in a mighty breath. And then Koko let out a scream. A magically enhanced bellow that was like a hurricane-force wind. It sent the soldiers soaring into the sky as if they were snowflakes. Jiho watched them turn into specks and vanish in the horizon. Without stopping her scream, Koko turned toward the gate, and her scream kicked up the debris from the exploded wall. She aimed it at Micah and Samena, who were now surrounded by a cloud of rubble and dust.

The danger was gone, but Koko could not stop. Jiho could see her face turning dangerously purple.

He ran and grabbed Koko, immediately stopping the scream and catching her as she collapsed into a dead faint.

"Good job, Jiho," his father said as he picked the princess up in his arms and ran for the exit. "Quickly! To the Kidahara!"

Only then did Jiho realize that his friends had been hurt. Both Calvin and Frankie were bleeding from different wounds, while Tess and Jay were helping Shane, who was limping.

Jiho ran over to support Calvin, who seemed dazed from a head wound.

"Thanks, Jiho," Calvin said. "I'm starting to see double now."

"I got you, friend," Jiho said. "Let's get you safe."

Supporting Calvin's weight on his shoulders, Jiho rushed them out of the east gate and into the thick forest of the Kidahara. As they ran, Jiho glanced over to see Micah and the Botan clan members lying among the cloud of rubble. But the fairy was gone.

Once they were in the Kidahara, Nackwon scouts

appeared and guided them to a cave entrance that was covered over with vines and hidden behind large bushes. Inside the cave, a hidden tunnel took the group into a vast cavern filled with several thousand soldiers. The scouts escorted them to Master Aeria's private tent, where all the other masters were already gathered.

"Master Remauld, thank the earth goddess that you all are safe! Were there any complications?" Aeria asked.

Remauld pointed at Ranger Park, who carried Koko into the tent and laid her down on a cot that was magicked.

"Iron poisoning," he said. "She used her powers, and it weakened her badly. But it was an amazing display of power. The strongest I've ever seen in a child so young."

Jiho felt terribly guilty.

"It was my fault," he blurted out. "I told her to use her magic even though she was so sick."

"Don't worry, young Park. The medics will come and take care of her," Aeria said. "She'll be fine after some rest."

But Jiho was concerned. Koko had never seemed weak before. She was always strong and vibrant and full of life. To see her so pale and lifeless felt so wrong. It made Jiho want to do something to help her. But what could he do? He didn't have any magic.

"We heard reports of a powerful fairy, Remauld," Master Diana demanded. "Did you recognize her?"

Remauld shook his head. "She calls herself Samena. I've

never seen her before, and yet there was something familiar about her."

"Samena? I don't know of any fairy by that name," Diana replied. "She must be a rogue fairy. Tell me everything you can about her."

As Remauld described the fairy and their altercation, Jiho remembered something strange.

"Master Remauld, when we were leaving I saw Micah, the bandit leader, knocked out on the ground, but not the fairy. There was no trace of her. She must have disappeared before the blast," Jiho said.

"Coward," Diana spit out. "Disappearing during a fight is cheating. She's probably no one of consequence."

"But I thought I saw a moonstone in Micah's hand," Jiho continued.

"What? Are you absolutely sure?" Diana asked sharply.

"Yes. I remember because it looked like a tiny moon. The other strange thing is that I remember seeing the fairy before."

"Where?"

"She was talking to the Omni Murtagh guy when I first joined them," Jiho said.

"Then she is in league with Luzee and her forces," Diana hissed. "We must find the moonstones and destroy them before they can set her free from the volcano."

"We know that there is one moonstone in Jinju," Remauld

said. "But it is useless without the other two, and no one knows where they are."

"The second moonstone is probably in Roku's hands by now," Zaki interrupted. "It was in the safekeeping of the king and queen of Joson."

"Then we have no time to lose," Diana said. "We must get them."

"Even if they have all three moonstones, they can't resurrect the staff of ki without Sejo's staff and a dragon's egg," Remauld said. "Moreover, even if they had the staff and the moonstones, they will never find another dragon's egg."

"Remauld, you are forgetting the power of those moonstones," Diana retorted. "They are the strongest of all fairy magic. When the first fairy queen felt herself fading from this world, she transferred her essence into the three moonstones that she harvested from moonlight and ocean spray. Then she became one with the wind. Because of the perversion created when Luzee made her staff of ki, the three moonstones completely bonded with Luzee and her magic. They may be enough to free her from the volcano."

Diana gazed bleakly at the others. "And then we would be doomed."

CHAPTER 20

IN THE PALACE receiving rooms that had become Roku's, Micah stood behind Samena as Prince Roku paced in front of them like a caged animal.

"She was here and you let her escape!" Roku seethed.

"She's not very far at all," Samena responded, with a languid wave of her slender pale hand. "I know exactly where she is."

"Then what are you waiting for? Bring her to me immediately!"

Samena stood very still. A stillness that was frightening in its malevolence. Micah didn't have to see her master's gaze to know what it looked like. The complete blanching of Roku's face let her know exactly how terrifying it was. Samena vanished and abruptly reappeared mere inches from Roku's face, causing the prince to lurch backward in fright.

"Do not forget who you speak to, Princeling," Samena said. "I am not a mortal at your beck and call."

"Terribly sorry, madam," Roku stuttered. "It is just that as long as she is free, my hold on the throne is tenuous."

"I don't care about your troubles," Samena said.

"But you should!" Roku retorted. "We made a deal. The princess in exchange for the moonstone."

Micah perked up. So Roku had the other moonstone. The sister to her own. *Then who has the third moonstone?* she wondered.

"What about my brother?" Micah asked.

"What about him?" Roku responded.

"Our deal was for me to get the princess to you, and you would release my brother. Now I want him freed."

"No, you were supposed to bring the princess directly to me!"

"Which I did! I brought her to your men, and your men lost her!"

"Micah's right," Samena replied. "She met her end of the deal. Release her brother. Now."

Samena's eyes glittered at Roku, and her fingertips lit up with electric sparks. Roku noted the threat immediately, and quickly ordered his men to release Micah's brother.

"And how are we going to get the princess back?" Roku demanded.

"We don't have to do anything," Samena said. "She will come to us. But she will not be alone."

Samena glided across the floor to gaze out the terrace windows at Mount Jiri.

"I adore this view," she drawled. "It reminds me of the old days. So kind of you to give me your rooms, Roku."

Staring at Roku until he stuttered his agreement, Samena floated toward the door.

"Come, Micah, let us make sure your brother is set free."

Micah scrambled to her feet and ran after her fairy master.

"My dearest girl, you are the only one I can trust," Samena said in her hypnotic voice. "The only one who is loyal to me; isn't that right, my pet?"

"Yes, my lady," Micah rushed to answer. "You can trust me completely."

The fairy stopped to smile at her young servant. "That is why only you can hold the moonstones for me. I cannot trust the others."

"The others? Do you know who has the third moonstone?" Micah asked.

"Yes, and it is on its way here. When it arrives, it is imperative that you take possession of both moonstones immediately."

Before Micah could ask another question, Mari appeared with Micah's brother, Kai, walking by her side.

"Micah!" Kai said in relief. "Thank the earth goddess! I can't believe you captured the princess!"

"We did, but the prince's stupid men let her escape," she said peevishly. "But that isn't our problem, Kai. The only thing I was worried about was saving you."

An unhappy look flitted across his face, surprising Micah.

"What, aren't you happy to see us?"

He recovered with a grateful smile. "No, of course! I'm so happy you were able to free me. It's just that I worry about what Roku will do to our clan, now that he doesn't have the princess."

"Nothing will happen to your clan as long as I am your benefactor," Samena cut in as she stepped forward into the light.

Kai's jaw dropped as he took in the fairy's extraordinary beauty. "My lady, I beg your pardon for not seeing you first," he said as he bowed deeply. "I am Kai Valon, Micah's older brother, and it is my honor to serve you,"

An unexpected surge of jealousy caught Micah by surprise as she watched her brother smooth-talk Samena.

Then, tearing her gaze away, she found Mari at her side, an anxious look on her weathered face.

"We've been away from the clan too long, Micah. We should return immediately," Mari said.

"Oh no, my dear one, Micah can't go home just yet," Samena interjected. "I need her. She is the only one I can trust."

"You can trust me too, my lady," Kai eagerly offered. "I will be your right-hand person."

Sharp anger stabbed Micah in the chest. "Mari, take Kai and go home. Now."

Kai faced Micah with an expression of hurt. "But I want to stay with you, Micah. You are my only sister. I can help you here. It is not a safe place for you to be alone."

She felt herself waver. When she was little, her brother used to take care of her, look after her. But he'd stopped once she became the White Peony. She missed the old days.

"Mari," Kai continued. "Don't you think you'd feel better if I stayed with Micah and you could go back and take care of the clan?"

"That's a wonderful idea," Samena offered. "We shouldn't keep Mari here when she is desperate to go home. Right, Micah?"

Micah nodded unhappily.

"Very well then, I shall leave you to your goodbyes," Samena said as she began to glide away.

"My lady, let me assist you!" Kai said, impulsively moving closer to the fairy. A bright explosion of sparks from Samena's arms sent Kai crashing to the ground.

"Kai, are you okay?" Micah asked in alarm.

Her dazed brother nodded. "I'm okay. It was just a shock."

"My apologies," Samena said. "I do not like anyone too close to me."

Kai jumped to his feet and bowed, promising it wouldn't happen again. He followed the fairy out, still apologizing. Micah stared after them, thinking of what she'd just seen. When Kai stepped close to Samena, right before the sparks, Micah had seen Samena flicker, as if she was a mirage. It was odd.

When they disappeared from sight, Mari let out a deep breath. "I don't like her," she whispered. "She's evil."

"You're wrong," Micah said. "She is the clan's savior."

"Or our undoing," Mari muttered. "Micah, please let's go home! Something bad is going to happen here. I feel it in my bones."

"Mari, go home. That's an order," Micah commanded. "Take the others and leave immediately."

The older woman let out a frustrated sigh. "Micah, I swear you're as stubborn as your mother. But you are still only a child. Listen to me. You are in over your head. You don't belong here. Leave the moonstone and come home. The clan needs you."

Micah shook off Mari's hand in irritation. "I'm not a child. I'm your clan leader, and I told you to go."

Without a backward glance, Micah marched away to find Samena. It bothered her to realize she was suspicious of her brother and his obvious desires to get close to the fairy. Was her brother trying to displace her? Would Samena choose Kai to hold the moonstones over Micah? Raw jealousy sent Micah running down the palace hallways seeking her fairy master again.

But as Micah entered Samena's receiving rooms, Brock

Murtagh arrived at that very moment, with what remained of his men.

"My lady, I have failed to make any progress in clearing the Kidahara," he said.

"My dear man," Samena drawled. "You were never meant to. I needed you as a distraction to flush the princess out. Which you did very well, thank you very much."

Murtagh looked stunned. "Do you mean all the money I wasted, all the men I lost? All that just to be a decoy for you?"

"Just a decoy? My dear, your role is critical to achieve our goal," Samena responded. "And once we are done, the Kidahara's resources will be yours to exploit."

Micah could see the greed light up the man's face. It filled her with disgust that her master would have to deal with such an unpleasant creature like him.

Now she understood why she was the only one Samena could trust. Looking over and seeing the avarice on even her brother's face made Micah feel protective of her fairy master. All these men who surrounded her only served her because they wanted something in return. Only Micah truly cared for Samena. Only Micah would do whatever she asked, with no expectation of any reward except for her master's approval.

CHAPTER 21

JIHO MET WITH his father as they went to check on the princess. His father stood in front of Koko's tent, leaning on his trusty staff. Jiho couldn't ever remember a moment where his father was without it. It was as much a part of him as his long, mane-like black hair. He remembered asking his father where he'd gotten the staff, and he had said that it was a family heirloom, passed down to the oldest Park for centuries. That it was their family's job to always keep it with them. Jiho thought it was bizarre. What was so special about an old wooden staff? It wasn't even interesting-looking. Just a very ancient, thick walking stick, with a big knobby head.

"What are you doing, Father?" Jiho asked.

His father shrugged. "I don't know why I feel so uneasy.

Staying close to the princess makes me feel a little better."

"But, Father, she's safe here, isn't she?"

"Yes, and yet I cannot quell my gut."

Jiho was concerned to hear this. While Jiho could sense danger right before it would hit, his father had always been able to sense trouble ahead of time. It was an instinct that he said came with being a Park. Now Jiho too began to feel troubled.

"You can both come in," Koko called out.

Inside, they found Master Aeria sitting by Koko's bedside.

"I've been having disturbing dreams," Koko was saying. "They all start with me in the castle. And then I see my parents, but it is only moments before a wave of lava engulfs them. Please, Master, we have to save them."

"We will, Princess," Aeria said soothingly. "Masters Remauld and Diana are working on a plan as we speak. You must be patient. The worst thing you can do is step foot in that castle again. It is what the enemy wants."

"But I want my parents back!" As the princess began to cry, namushin came scurrying into the room to soothe her. Their soft murmuring voices lulled the princess to sleep as they tucked themselves all around her.

Aeria gestured for Jiho and his father to step outside.

"Aeria," Ranger Park said. "I sense more trouble is coming."

"I do too," Aeria replied. "It would make me feel better if both of you were to stay near the princess at all times."

"Of course," Ranger Park said with a deep bow.

Jiho bowed also.

"What kind of trouble are you worried about?" Jiho asked when they were alone.

His father tapped his staff on the ground before leaning on it. "The nightwalkers were the first omen. They only ever come out when dark days are coming. It means there is a disturbance in our worlds. If we are not careful, we will enter a time when nightwalkers will roam free and humans will live in hiding."

A vision of the horrific nightwalkers flashed before Jiho's eyes and he shuddered.

"What are we supposed to do?" he asked his father.

Ranger Park stood staring at his wooden staff for a long moment.

"Jiho, you are a Park. By blood that makes you a ranger of the Kidahara. If anyone knows the forest, it is you. The namushin already trust you. But if something ever happens to me, you must promise me to protect the princess. And you must promise me that you will claim my staff and not let anyone take it from you."

His father's gaze was so intense that Jiho backed away nervously.

"Promise me, Jiho."

"Yeah, okay. I promise," Jiho agreed.

Only then did his father's gaze lighten.

"We should both stay here and keep watch," he said.

Jiho nodded. For the first time, he was starting to

understand why his father had left his family. It wasn't just the Kidahara that was in danger. It was their entire world.

Later that evening, Jiho sat staring at the mating dance of glowing rhino beetles as his father slept beside him. He'd spent the night carving a large tree branch into his own version of his father's staff. Jiho had never liked the sword his friends had given him and didn't know how to wield it. But after seeing the violence on the streets of Jinju, he felt the need to have a weapon. He'd been lucky enough to run into Master Remauld, who'd magicked a piece of black ironwood for him. It was the hardest and strongest wood in the Kidahara. Jiho had carved it into a formidable staff with a heavy knobbed head, and polished it until it shone. He was proud of his staff.

"You should still carry a sword with you also," Remauld had said.

Jiho thought that was a bad idea. He would rather carry his slingshot instead. He had better control with his little slingshot than with a big heavy sword that could be used against him.

Suddenly, he heard the distressed murmuring of the namushin from within Koko's tent before she appeared before him.

"Koko, what are you doing up?" Jiho asked in surprise.

But she did not respond. Her eyes were wide-open and unblinking as they stared sightlessly ahead. The namushin rushed over to Jiho, and he caught the urgency of their concern as the princess began to walk away from them.

"Koko!" Jiho tried to stop her, when his father pushed him away.

"Don't touch her, Jiho," his father said. "She has been enchanted. We don't know what sort of spell or curse she is under."

"But won't we nullify the spell?" Jiho asked.

"Yes, but we don't know at what cost," his father replied. His eyebrows furrowed with worry. "We could cancel the magic and trap her in a coma forever or it could kill her. We can't risk it."

They quickly followed beside her.

"What do we do?"

"The only thing we can do. Follow her and keep her safe."

Ranger Park leaned down to address the distressed namushin. "Go and tell all the masters what is happening. We will stay with her."

The little namushin scurried away as Jiho stayed by Koko's side. She walked steadily but purposefully through the great cavern. The first to arrive was Master Remauld. He immediately created a solid concrete wall that he placed in her path. The princess stopped upon reaching it. She put her hands against the wall, and magic flew out of her, disintegrating the wall into rubble. Koko stepped over the rubble and kept walking.

"She's heading for Jinju. Why can't we magic her back to

Mir, where she'll be safe?" Jiho asked.

"Any attempt of magic on her is dangerous," Aeria said as she appeared by his side. "It could kill her. There is no safe way to stop her. We must go along."

"This is obviously a trap for us," Diana said as she and Master Zaki and his namushin arrived by Aeria's side.

"Yes, no doubt," Aeria said. "Wait for my signal and be prepared for a battle."

The three other masters bowed and disappeared. Koko had reached the tunnel's end and was now out in the dark woods. The evening sky lit up with the bright light of the moon and the myriad of stars that sparkled above them. Koko's eyes never strayed from the path before her. She didn't trip or misstep. She walked as surely as if she were completely aware of where she was going. And yet, the vacant expression on her face made clear that she was not there.

Jiho tried talking to her, entreating her to stop. But nothing worked. She kept her steady pace toward the city walls. Once at the east gate, Koko pushed open the heavy oak doors with a single-arm motion. There was no one stationed there. The streets were completely empty and eerily quiet.

The steady steps of the princess echoed loudly as she walked. Aeria turned to Ranger Park. "I will go ahead to see where the danger lies," she said.

Jiho's father nodded, and Aeria vanished.

"Do you get the feeling we are being watched, son?"

Jiho nodded. Since the moment they entered the gate into Jinju, he'd felt the creepy sensation of hundreds of eyes watching him. And the intensity of the feeling grew stronger as they followed Koko down the darkened streets of Jinju. Every block, Jiho jumped upon seeing a shadow, until they were halfway to the castle and a large shadow moved across the street before them.

As the princess kept walking, the light of a single moonbeam fell across a large, massive bulk. Jiho almost screamed, but his father covered his mouth with his hand.

"Don't show your fear," he whispered to Jiho.

"But that thing is going to eat us!" Jiho loudly whispered back.

Trying to swallow his panic, Jiho bit his lips as the monster lurched into full view. It was a massive praying mantis, which reared up on its powerful back legs. As it towered over them, it lowered its head so they could see its huge, bulging compound eyes and razor-sharp mandibles.

"How did Master Aeria not see this thing?" Jiho asked.

Koko had stopped walking when the creature appeared, but then proceeded right into the giant monster's path. Jiho raced forward and whacked the praying mantis hard on the face as it lunged at Koko. It let out a piercing shriek and tried to stab him with its many sharp front legs. As Jiho danced backward, leading the gigantic insect away from the princess, his father climbed on top of its back and began to smash it hard on its head. The monster bucked fiercely, trying to throw its tormentor off, but Ranger Park held fast.

"Jiho, we need to rip its antennae off!"

With no time to waste, Jiho seized his slingshot and several sharp rocks from his pocket and sent off a dozen shots into the massive compound eye. The creature let out an ear-piercing scream of pain and lunged at Jiho, stabbing its legs into the ground so hard it became stuck. Racing forward, Jiho caught hold of a flailing antenna and heaved with all his might, ripping it out of the creature's head. Before it could move, Ranger Park had climbed all the way to its head and, seizing the other antenna, jumped off, flipping it onto its back.

The giant praying mantis squirmed on the ground, gnashing its mandibles vainly at them. It turned its antenna-less head around and around, but it could not right itself.

"The princess!" Ranger Park raced after Koko while Jiho ran on shakier legs. He was relieved to see that she was fine, but still under the enchantment. They were now getting close to the castle.

"Where is Master Aeria?" Jiho asked.

"Hopefully she's not hurt," his father said.

"I'd like not to be hurt either," Jiho said. "I wonder what is coming next."

And soon, his answer came flying down from the roofs above them. Stone gargoyles. A dozen of them. They were small and mean, gray with grotesque faces and bat-like wings.

The first two tried to grab the princess, but Ranger Park stepped forward and grabbed the gargoyles by the wings, immediately turning them into stone and letting them smash to the ground.

"Be careful, son," Ranger Park warned. "They're really fast and vicious!"

Jiho ran forward and punched a gargoyle in the nose. It grunted right before transforming into its statue form. Jiho whirled around and hit several more that tried to sneak up on him. One snatched him by his hair and tried to fly off with him. Jiho grabbed its legs and he had to quickly roll out of the way when the stone gargoyle crashed. But every time one gargoyle petrified, five more would appear.

"It's no good!" Jiho yelled as they circled them. "There're too many."

He was getting exhausted, but he couldn't let up, trying his best to match his father, who was a fighting machine. But even his father was overwhelmed. He was nearly buried in a pile of a dozen gargoyle statues that had attacked him, separating him from the princess.

One finally got a hold of the princess and began lifting her into the air.

"*No!*" Jiho shouted as he launched himself at the gargoyle, sending them crashing to the ground. Koko lay motionless by his side. More gargoyles were coming as Jiho positioned himself in front of the princess.

And then a blinding light shone down from the sky,

sending the gargoyles shrieking. When Jiho opened his eyes, he saw many of the gargoyles frozen into statues, while the rest were scurrying into the shadows.

Master Aeria lowered her staff.

"My apologies for the delay," she said.

"You came just in time," Ranger Park said.

"Actually, a little earlier would have been more helpful," Jiho corrected.

"And a little later would have been far worse," Aeria retorted. "But it seems these diversions were just to get rid of the two of you."

"It almost worked," Jiho said.

"Well, they've lured us this far. Do you know how they will entrap us?" Ranger Park asked.

"No, I could not see into the castle," Aeria said. "But we will find out shortly."

Koko had reached the castle stairs and had begun to climb.

"But how can we blindly go in, knowing it's a trap?" Jiho asked.

"I will not leave Princess Koko's side," Aeria said gently. "But remember, you and your father's unique and secret talents may be our only chance to save her."

Unable to argue against this, Jiho remained quiet. The climb to the castle felt excruciatingly long. At the castle entrance, the doors were open but unmanned. They stepped inside an empty hall and followed the princess to the throne room. The room was empty except for two large bejeweled thrones in the front of the room. Their reflections stared back at them from the mirrors covering every wall of the room. In the middle of the room, Koko finally stopped.

Master Aeria stood in front of the princess and spoke to the empty room.

"We are here, as you wanted," she said. "Show yourself."

A figure materialized, sitting on one of the thrones.

"That's the fairy Samena," Jiho said to Aeria.

"And you are the Grand Council Master Aeria, the greatest witch of all the Kidahara," Samena said. "Welcome."

"I am here to ask you to release the princess from your enchantment," Aeria said.

"I would be happy to do so," Samena said. "As soon as the other masters show themselves. I would like a proper introduction."

The fairy smiled with such malice that Jiho could not ignore the gut-churning warnings that flooded his system.

"They will come only if you release the princess," Aeria said.

"Then we are at an impasse," Samena drawled. "What a pity. The longer the princess stays in this particular spell, the greater the chance that she will never be free."

Frustrated, Aeria slammed her cane on the ground with a resounding thud that echoed throughout the hall. "You must give us some reassurance that you will release the princess."

Jiho shifted nervously as a tense silence lengthened.

"Oh, very well," Samena said. With a snap of her fingers, the doors behind her opened, and several people entered the room. Jiho recognized the bandit leader, the Omni Murtagh boss man, and Prince Roku. There was one other man who entered, but Jiho didn't know who he was.

Samena pointed at Micah and the unknown man. "This is Micah and Kai Valon of the Botan clan. They are my loyal servants. You may hold them hostage."

The two Botan clan members walked across the room to stand behind Aeria.

"What kind of trickery is this?" Ranger Park muttered.

Jiho agreed. But he knew there was not much they could do. He shot an evil glare at Micah, who avoided his gaze. Jiho would never trust her or any of her Botan clan members again.

"Now, bring the other masters here, before you lose the princess forever."

The Grand Council Master called out in a ringing voice. "Masters of the Nackwon Council, come to me now!"

Upon her words, Masters Remauld, Diana, and Zaki appeared.

"Who are you?" Master Diana asked, her eyes narrowed on the fairy sitting on the throne. "You look familiar. How do I know you?"

"It's a surprise," Samena said with a teeth-baring smile.

"I have done as you have asked. Now release the princess," Aeria commanded.

"Very well," Samena said. She opened her hand and an object flew toward them. It floated in the air until it fell at their feet. It was a large purple flower with long black hairs wrapped tightly around it.

Jiho started to pick it up, but Master Aeria stopped him. "We have to release the hairs from the flower without damaging it."

"Can't you use magic?" he asked.

Aeria shook her head. "No, we cannot use magic on this enchantment. We must do it by hand. If we damage the flower, we risk trapping the princess forever."

"Let me do it," Zaki said. Carefully picking up the flower, the master slowly but nimbly unraveled Koko's hairs from the petals until it was completely free. At that moment, Koko let out a loud gasp and stumbled forward.

"Where am I?"

As soon as Koko was free from the spell, the masters moved to attack Samena, yet nothing happened. There was no magic.

The fairy laughed as the mirrored walls of the room began to close in. The masters were stunned as servants entered the room and pushed away the mirrored walls, revealing iron bars.

"The room was the trap," Diana spit out. "You've killed us all, Aeria!"

Soldiers marched in with iron chains that they placed on the Nackwon Council masters and Koko. Jiho caught Koko as she fell.

"Koko, I've got you," he said. "Lean on me."

But then he caught sight of his father fighting off the soldiers, refusing to give up his staff. Jiho saw a soldier readying his weapon to shoot.

"No, Papa!" Jiho shouted. "No!"

Everything happened in slow motion. He let go of Koko and started to run to his father. An explosive gunshot rang through Jiho's ears, rocking him on his feet. He stumbled and saw the shock on his father's face and then the large bright red flower blossoming on his chest.

"Papa!" Jiho was sobbing as he fell to his knees, trying desperately to stop the blood that flowed steadily.

"My staff," his father whispered. His shaking hand still tried to hold on as the soldiers wrenched it from his grasp.

"Papa, no!" Jiho couldn't stop the bleeding. "Please someone help me!"

He looked wildly all around him. He could see Koko's devastated face as she cried in Aeria's arms. Master Remauld tried to approach but was jerked back onto his knees by the soldier holding his chains. Both Masters Zaki and Diana looked on helplessly as they were being pulled away, out of the room. It was the bandit leader who knelt down by his side and took a look at the wound.

"We have to see if there is an exit wound," she said. Gently, she lifted Ranger Park up to look at his back. "There isn't one, so we have to keep pressure on it. Press tightly." She placed a cloth on top of the wound and pressed Jiho's hands on top of the cloth. "I'll go get some medicine to stop the bleeding."

She jumped up to her feet as her brother grabbed her arm.

"Micah, what are you doing?" Kai asked.

"I can't just let him die," she said.

"They're not our concern. You're upsetting my lady."

Micah looked back to see Samena gazing at her with a slight smile on her face. "She's fine," she answered curtly. "Her main goal was getting his staff, not killing him."

And with that she left.

"Teacher," Koko cried brokenly. She tried to cover her face but was pulled painfully to her feet by her guards.

"You promised to release the princess!" Aeria raged.

"No, no, no. I promised to release her from the dreamwalk," Samena replied. "I never promised to release her completely. Why would I do that? I need her."

Prince Roku, who had been silent next to Samena, now sat on the throne next to her. "I am the king," he pronounced, as a manic smile spread across his face.

Samena ignored him and ordered the guards to take the prisoners to the dungeons. The masters were all badly affected by the iron, but Koko could hardly walk. Unrelenting, the guards dragged them out by the chains as Micah returned, holding a basket of bandages and jars.

She knelt by Ranger Park's side and listened to his breathing before gently moving Jiho's hands away for a moment.

"It doesn't look like the bullet hit his lungs, which was my major concern. And the bleeding has slowed down."

She opened a few jars and mixed several sharp-smelling ointments together in a small cup.

"What is that?" Jiho asked. "It's not magic, is it?"

Micah snorted. "People like to pretend that this is magic, but it is just good old folk medicine using herbs and some mountain roots and a secret Botan clan ingredient. This will stop the bleeding and keep the wound from getting infected."

"Will he be all right?" Jiho asked.

"If you keep his wound clean and watch over him," she said.

Micah moved the cloth from the wound and quickly applied the paste, then covered it with a new bandage. She added several padded layers before wrapping the last bandage over and around Ranger Park's shoulder to keep it in place.

As soon as she was done, the guards slapped manacles on Jiho's hands and placed Ranger Park on a stretcher.

"Be careful with him," she admonished sharply.

As they led them away, Jiho turned to look back at Micah. "Thank you," he said.

CHAPTER 22

MICAH COULDN'T QUELL the strange feeling that sat in the pit of her stomach. She'd had it ever since entering the castle, and it had worsened since the imprisonment of the Nackwon Council masters. When she was with Samena, she was so enthralled by her mere presence that she could ignore the feeling. But away from the fairy, Micah couldn't ignore the sense that something was desperately wrong.

Seeing her master Samena give the order to shoot the ranger solely to get his staff had been eye-opening. The callous disregard for life, by her brother even, had shocked Micah. She wanted to talk to Kai, find out what had changed him. But he was always by Samena's side.

And Samena herself seemed off to Micah. The strong connection that Micah had felt with the fairy had faded.

Had Kai supplanted her in Samena's affections?

Now she deeply regretted not leaving with Mari when the others had. She missed Mari and her wise counsel desperately. Yet she knew Samena wouldn't have let her go. Would Samena still trust her with the moonstones, or had she lost faith in her number one?

But the real question was, would Micah follow through on what Samena wanted her to do? Having seen what had happened today, Micah didn't know what she would do. The Botan clan had always been about protecting the weak from the powerfully corrupt. What was she doing here helping a powerful fairy who was seeking absolute power? Was she betraying generations of White Peony chiefs by choosing to side with Samena and Roku?

What Samena planned to do would lead to a new world with a new leader. Yet it would come at the expense of much death and destruction. Micah could finally see that now, and it frightened her deeply.

Chapter 23

On their way down to the dungeons, Jiho kept a close eye on the guards carrying his father. He yelled when the guards almost dropped him down the narrow stairway and earned himself a sharp smack on the head.

The cells were dark, with only small horizontal slivers that let a little of the natural light inside. The sun had risen, and the few rays that shone through only highlighted the filthy conditions. Six cells had been built in a big circle. The guards dropped Jiho's father unceremoniously on the floor of the last open cell and locked the door. Jiho cursed as his father moaned in pain. As he knelt on the filthy floor, Jiho was at least grateful that they'd left his father on the stretcher.

"Jiho, how's your father?" Aeria asked from the cell across the way.

"I don't know," he replied. "He seems stable for now."

He stood up to look out through his prison bars and saw Aeria and Zaki in one cell and Remauld and Diana in the cell next to them. Diana looked livid and was talking in hushed tones to Remauld, all while glaring at Jiho.

At the other end, across from the staircase and to Jiho's right, was the largest cell, where Koko was being embraced by her parents. The king and queen looked gaunt and exhausted, but so happy to see their daughter. Yet Jiho could see that Koko was not doing well.

"Princess, are you all right?"

Koko raised her head slightly and gave Jiho a weak smile. "I'm fine because I'm with my parents. At last."

The queen wiped away her tears to smile at her daughter. "We've been so worried about you."

The king stood up and walked over to the bars. "Why is she so weak? What has happened to her?"

"It's the iron shackles," Jiho said. "This is her second time being exposed to iron, and she was already really sick from it before."

"What do we do? How can we help her?" the king asked.

Master Zaki, who had been very quiet, came to the front of his cell to speak to the king.

"Your Majesty, iron poisoning can be deadly for magic folk. The only cure for her is to get out of those shackles."

The queen gasped in horror, and the king shook the cell bars in fury.

It reminded Jiho of how he'd felt while trapped in the iron wagon.

"Princess, you need to hold my hand," Jiho said. He moved to the farthest corner of his cell and reached his arm into the neighboring cell. "I can help you! Remember the wagon? I nullify magic, so the iron can't hurt you."

The king quickly lifted Koko and brought her as close as possible to grab Jiho's hand. Several minutes passed and Koko's grip on his hand grew stronger.

"Thank you, Jiho," she said. "I feel better already. But your arm must be so tired."

"It's okay," he said. "But maybe we should sit, so your father doesn't have to hold you the whole time."

"I could hold you forever, my little Koko," the king replied.

Koko giggled. "Thanks, Papa."

"How is that possible?" Diana asked. "Why isn't the iron affecting his magic like it is doing to all of us?"

"It is strange," Zaki mused.

Only Remauld let out a quiet laugh. "Of course! His essence is to nullify magic, which is what iron does. But Jiho's talent only manifests itself when magic is directed at him. So the iron has nothing to nullify."

The princess and Jiho sat holding hands for a long while before Koko finally let go. "I'm feeling a lot better now," she said. "Why don't you check on your dad and rest your arm for a while."

Jiho stood in relief and stretched.

He went over to check on his father, who was still sleeping. He wished there was a blanket for his dad, but there was nothing in the cell. Frustrated, he returned to the corner to help Koko again.

"I wonder what they're talking about," Koko said.

Jiho looked to see the masters huddled together whispering through their cell bars. Their discussion was becoming agitated until finally Diana pulled away.

"Jiho," Diana yelled from her cell. "Why didn't you or your father tell us that he had Sejo's staff? It was part of Luzee's staff of ki!"

"What in the world are you talking about?" Jiho asked, perplexed by her fury.

"Wait, your father's walking stick was Sejo's staff?" Koko asked in surprise. "Remember the pool of dragon's tears in Mir? It showed us how Luzee created the staff of ki with the three most powerful magical objects—the dragon's egg, the three moonstones, and Chief Wizard Sejo's staff."

Gaping in surprise, Jiho responded heatedly. "We had no idea what it was!"

"How could you not know you held one of the most powerful magical artifacts in the world?" Diana blasted at him.

"Because it's just an old walking staff that's been passed down in my family for generations."

"Just an old walking staff? The nerve—" Diana cut in.

"Well, if it was so important, why didn't you guys

recognize it?" Jiho yelled back. "You should've known what it was as soon as you saw it!"

Diana was momentarily speechless. "How dare you!" she yelled.

But before she could continue, Remauld calmed her down. "Stop, Diana, he's right. They didn't know. How could they? They're not Nackwon Council members. But we should have known that the Parks would have been tasked with keeping it safe. After all, their ability is to nullify magic. What better way to hide the most important magical artifact in all of Nackwon but to give it to them? None of us could see what it was."

"But then how did Samena recognize it?" Diana asked.

Neither Aeria nor Remauld had an answer to her question. But Jiho remembered when he'd first seen her. She'd said something he'd thought was strange.

You also have something that I need. Something that used to be mine. And now I want it back.

"She knew what it was," Jiho said. "She told my father he had something of hers. It had to have been the staff."

"How could she have known?" Aeria asked. "Even Remauld didn't recognize it."

"She had to have seen the staff of ki personally," Diana commented. "Which would mean . . ."

"She was there when Luzee first created it," Remauld finished.

"Who is she?"

"Clearly a disciple of Luzee who we were unaware of," Aeria said darkly. "And she is trying to free her."

"What can we do?"

"We have to stop her," Aeria said. "We have to escape from here. We have to hope that even if she frees Luzee, she cannot rebuild the staff of ki without a dragon's egg."

"If she frees Luzee, then we are all in danger, whether she rebuilds it or not," Diana said grimly. "Sejo's staff and the moonstones combined are still more powerful than any other magical object we have in our arsenal. We don't know the true limit of its power."

The atmosphere was tense as the masters fell quiet. Jiho could see that the iron was visibly weakening all of them. He felt so helpless and lost. Jiho gazed at his father, lying so still. If only he wasn't hurt. Ranger Park was the strongest man he knew. Iron didn't affect him either. His father would've been able to break them out of this jail. He would've come up with a plan to help them.

At that moment, Koko squeezed Jiho's hand, reminding him that she was there, and he was not alone. Jiho drew in a shaky breath. They had to think of something. They had no choice.

CHAPTER 24

MICAH WATCHED AS the other sycophants plied Samena with gushing praise and flattery. The receiving room was filled with them: Roku and his loathsome minions, the Omni Murtagh employees and the repulsive Brock Murtagh. All fawning over Samena as they realized the power dynamic in the room. Yet the fairy was indifferent to them all, gazing out the open veranda doors to the view of Mount Jiri. They still fought for her attention like flies at a dung heap. And the worst of them all was her brother. He never left Samena's side. Micah was sure that Kai would lick the soles of Samena's feet but for the fact that no one was allowed to touch her. And how odd was that? Micah had always wondered why Samena never touched her, not even accidentally. She wouldn't even take the moonstone from Micah's hands.

In fact, she had never seen the fairy pick up anything with her hands.

How strange it was.

The moonstones that Samena so desperately desired but needed Micah to collect, protect, and hold in her bag. With the admonishment to keep them with her at all times. If they were so important to her, why wouldn't she at least want to see them, examine them, touch them? Why had she relied on Micah to take back the moonstones from Roku and Murtagh?

It was puzzling.

Now watching the fairy without the rosy glow of infatuation that had once tinged her views, Micah noticed the subtle nuances she'd missed before. The slight shimmer that surrounded Samena meant she had protected herself with magic. It made her seem unreal, as if she were a mirage, an illusion. What was the fairy so afraid of? She said she trusted Micah, but clearly the truth was that she trusted no one. What would happen if Micah left with the moonstones?

As if sensing Micah's thoughts, Samena's unnaturally blue eyes settled on her. She beckoned her over with one finger, and Micah was compelled to join her.

"You are unhappy, my dearest," Samena said. "Tell me what is the matter."

"Micah has always been an angry little child," Kai chimed in with a smarmy smile. "Nothing makes her happy, even when she has everything."

Micah closed her eyes, biting back the nasty retort forming on the tip of her tongue. She'd saved her brother from imprisonment—she thought that at least their family bonds kept them unified. But lately, she wondered if she was looking and hoping for something that was not really there. It reminded her of how her brother had changed after she'd inherited the White Peony title. The older brother who had always looked out for her and took care of her seemed to transform overnight. The truth that she never wanted to acknowledge was so obvious now.

"Go away, my pet," Samena said to Kai, shooing him with a languid wave of her pale hand.

Shock and then anger showed on Kai's face. The glare he shot Micah saddened her. Had he always hated her this much?

"Micah, you have not been yourself," Samena said. "What is it?"

Micah stared into the fairy's cold blue eyes and wondered why she ever thought they were kind and caring. How had she missed the cold calculation in the flatness of her eyes, the cruelty in the curve of the fairy's beautiful lips? Micah could feel evil as if it was a tangible thing. She suppressed a shudder, and self-preservation kicked in.

"You only pay attention to Kai," Micah complained. "You seem to like him more than me! But I'm the one who helped you, not Kai. He hasn't done anything for you!"

The coldness in Samena's eyes changed to amused tolerance.

"I am sorry, my dearest," Samena cooed. "I didn't realize you were feeling so jealous and left out. But do not fret. Everything will be different after tonight. And you will be by my side and handsomely rewarded."

Micah recognized the command in her words. Fear flickered through her as she thought of the princess and the masters locked up in the dungeon below.

What had she done?

Chapter 25

It was nighttime when the guards finally returned. They'd stopped by at midday briefly to drop off bread and water. But now, they returned with orders to take the prisoners directly to Samena.

"What about my father?" Jiho asked.

"We're to bring him up also."

Now Jiho knew why they'd left him on the stretcher.

The guards pushed and prodded them all the way up to what used to be the king and queen's private receiving rooms. Inside, they found Prince Roku lounging on a new and ostentatious throne. Brock Murtagh and Kai stood on either side of him. The guards left them in the center of the room and retreated to the back wall.

"Hello, dear brother," Roku said with a smirk.

Jiho could feel the waves of rage coming from the king.

"I have no brother," King Suri said.

"Well, technically, half brother," Roku said. "But once you're dead, we won't have to worry about little details like that."

"You can kill me, but leave Yuna and Koko out of this," King Suri pleaded. "Let them go."

"What? But then I would be an illegitimate king! I can't have that."

"They'll renounce all claims to the throne of Joson," King Suri said. "They will say it publicly and swear allegiance to you as king."

"No! Never!" Koko yelled. "I'd rather die!"

"Well, that solves that problem!" Roku laughed. "You can all die together!"

The large double doors leading out to the veranda opened with a gust of wind.

"Not so fast," Samena said. Micah walked beside her, carrying Ranger Park's staff in her hand. But no longer did it look like an old walking stick. It was longer and darker and seemed to pulse with energy. But why, Jiho wondered, was Micah carrying such a powerful weapon that she could not have possibly wielded? Why was Samena not protecting it herself?

"I need an audience for the festivities tonight," Samena drawled.

Roku leaped to his feet and bowed obsequiously. "Your throne, my lady."

Samena ignored him and stood in front of the masters. "You are not looking so well," she said with a toothy grin. "Too much iron in your diet?"

Roku, Murtagh, and Kai laughed uproariously. Only Micah remained unsmiling. Jiho stared at the bandit leader, knowing he couldn't trust her and yet hoping she would surprise him once again.

"Enough of that," Samena said, waving the others quiet. "It is time to right an ancient wrong. It is time to free your master. Come, Micah, let us begin."

Micah stepped forward and held the staff in front of her. Samena electrified it with her hands so that it began to float in the air, revolving slowly.

"Place the moonstones on the staff of ki," Samena commanded.

Micah opened her bag, revealing the three moonstones.

"Don't do it, Micah," Koko yelled. "She's going to release L—"

But before Koko could finish, Samena shot a spell that sealed all of their mouths shut. Jiho looked around to see that they were all affected but him. Should he say something? Should he finish Koko's sentence? Before he could say anything, he caught Remauld's warning eye and remembered his words.

In a war of magic, your talent could be the difference between victory and annihilation.

Jiho stayed quiet.

"Micah, what are you waiting for? Place the moonstones on the staff of ki!"

With shaking hands, Micah placed the first moonstone into a cavity around the head of the staff. The moonstone clicked into place and began to shine brightly. She did the same for the second and the third one. With the final one locked into place, the staff began to let out a low hum.

"Now bring the princess forward," Samena said.

Jiho bit his tongue to keep from protesting as the guards dragged Koko away from her parents, who fought vigorously.

Samena snapped her fingers, and the silence spell was lifted as the queen's scream suddenly filled the room.

"It's no fun if I can't hear you scream," Samena said. "Now, Micah, the dagger."

Micah slowly pulled out a strange dagger. Its blade was black and not straight but wavy, with a wicked point. The guards held Koko's arm over the staff as Micah approached with the dagger held high.

"That blade has been made with dark magic," Master Zaki whispered to Jiho. "It is going to hurt the princess terribly."

Samena chanted in an ancient, unrecognizable language. The lights flickered and mist formed in the room all around them. She chanted louder, and Jiho could swear he heard the echo of voices chanting along. The moonstones began to pulse in rhythm. Samena then nodded at Micah, but the bandit leader froze.

"Now, Micah, you must release her blood!"

"Don't do it, Micah! You're not that evil," Jiho yelled. "Please don't hurt Koko!"

Micah's hand was trembling so hard she dropped the knife and gasped.

"I can't, I can't," she sobbed. "I'm so sorry, Princess."

With a furious howl, Samena blasted Micah across the room, where she crumbled to the floor in a heap.

"You fool, I should have known you'd be too weak."

She turned to the others. "Which one of you will prove their worth to me tonight?"

It was Kai who leaned down and grabbed the dagger, approaching the frightened princess. Samena began to chant again. This time there was a wildness to the response. Jiho could hear the echoes of many voices, but he had no idea where they were coming from. The moonstones pulsed frantically, and Samena screamed, "Now!"

Kai sliced Koko's palm, and blood poured onto the top of the staff and formed the shape of an egg. Koko moaned in pain.

"Great earth goddess, she has resurrected the staff of ki," Aeria whispered.

"We have lost," Diana cried.

On top of the staff was a perfectly formed dragon's egg made of blood.

The staff of ki rose in the air and landed on the floor with a loud bang. Everyone but Samena fell back as a hurricane-force wind emanated from the staff. And then an answering explosion sounded from outside. They all turned to look out over the veranda and were stunned to see that Mount Jiri was erupting. Lava spewed from the top, and a figure could be seen flying out of the erupting volcano. The figure had large wings and began flying toward the castle at a rapid speed.

"Here comes the empress," Samena crowed.

"It's Luzee," Diana said.

Jiho crawled over to Micah. "If you can hear me, please help us."

Micah didn't move.

While everyone was absorbed in watching the coming figure, Jiho next crawled over to Koko and dragged her away from the staff of ki.

"We've got to get you out of here," he whispered.

Koko looked dazed and sick. "It's too late," she said. "There's nothing we can do."

"That's not true," Jiho said sharply.

Something poked at him, and Jiho turned to see that Micah had snuck over.

"Cover me while I pick this lock," she said. She held two long thin metal pieces in her hands, and she immediately began to work on Koko's manacles. Within seconds, she had Koko's arms free and then her legs. As she worked on Jiho's locks, he stared anxiously at the princess.

"Her wound won't stop bleeding," Jiho whispered.

Micah pulled a bag from her pocket and rubbed a thick green paste on Koko's palm. "I was going to give this to you for your dad," she said. "It stops the bleeding." She then wrapped a fresh bandage over Koko's hand.

"I know it's late, but for what it's worth, I'm real sorry," Micah said.

"I know," Koko said. "And thank you."

"We don't have time for that," Jiho interrupted. "Koko, you need to find your dragon magic now. This is your chance."

Koko looked terrified, but she nodded. "I'll try."

But before she could do anything, the flying figure landed with a large thud on the veranda. It was tall with a tremendous wingspan, and its shape was caked in volcanic ash. Every step it took, it left a pile of soot and dark residue on the ground. It walked into the room, and its piercing silver eyes fixated on the staff of ki floating before the frozen figure of Samena.

"What is wrong with Samena?" Micah whispered, before being quickly shushed by Jiho.

The ash-covered figure grasped the staff between both its hands, crooning to it. "I have missed you, my love." Its voice was deep and hoarse from centuries of neglect. "Now let's make things right again."

Holding the staff high in the air, it began to chant, "Staff of ki, change my fate, return me to my beauteous shape."

A blinding light flashed across the room and then a rippling wave of prismatic lights shot out from the staff. The wave of light undulated between Samena and the ash-covered figure. Samena began to glow, as if a small sun was within her. It grew brighter and brighter until she exploded in a shower of light particles that flew into the ash-covered figure, where it was completely absorbed and pulsed from within.

"By my ancestor's grave, she *is* Samena!" Micah said as she, Jiho, and Koko watched the transformation. "Quick, we must hide!"

She pulled Jiho and Koko toward the back of the room and out onto the veranda.

"What do you mean by that?" Koko asked.

Micah kept gazing back at the scene behind them. "I always thought it was odd how Samena could never touch anything. And she would flicker, as if she were not real but a mirage of some kind. But now it's clear. She was never real. She was just a projection of—"

The figure slammed the staff against the floor, and the light that filled it began to pulse, brighter and brighter, until it too exploded into a shower of electric sparks and revealed a new being. A fairy with bright silver hair and steel-gray eyes and skin the color of fallen snow. But her large, feathered wings were jet-black, and no longer the pale gray they once were.

Luzee had returned.

Her glorious wings spread behind her and flapped down hard, letting out a powerful gust of wind that knocked everyone off their feet. She threw back her head and laughed, her voice hoarse and full of malevolence. Her glittering eyes stared at the masters and she smiled.

"I'm back!"

CHAPTER 26

"WHERE IS SAMENA?" Roku asked peevishly. "And who are you?"

"I am your ruler," Luzee replied. "Bow down to me."

Roku looked offended. "I am a king! I do not bow down to anyone. I had a pact with Samena. Where is she?"

"Samena is no more, there is only Luzee," the fairy remarked. "Now bow down to me, little man."

"I will do no such thing," Roku sniped. Before he could say another word, Luzee threw out her hand toward him, shooting out a large bolt of electricity that killed him instantly. Roku's body fell to the ground, his blackened face and staring eyes on display for everyone to see. An instant lesson of Luzee's power and ruthlessness.

Those who were not already on the floor fell down and

genuflected. Only the Nackwon Council masters rose to their feet to face Luzee fearlessly.

"I knew there was something familiar about that Samena character," Diana said with a smirk. "She reeked of a familiar foulness."

"Hello, sister," Luzee said with a toothy smile identical to Samena's.

"You are no sister of mine," Diana spat.

"Well then, it won't hurt me to kill you."

Luzee summoned her magic to drag Diana into the air by her throat, her feet dangling as she pulled her toward the staff. The blood egg glowed a dark red as the moonstones pulsed rhythmically. "Your power is mine," Luzee hissed. She touched the egg to Diana's forehead, causing her to scream. From her open mouth, a blue amorphous light appeared. It was long and curled like smoke above Diana's head. Luzee's eyes lit up with avaricious delight, and she breathed in the blue tendrils. Diana began to choke and fight, but the light continued to drift slowly out of her body. With every breath Luzee inhaled, Diana's form grew limper, and her once-vibrant complexion turned sallow. Her cheeks hollowed out and her eyes bulged out of their sockets, leaving her like a skeletal version of her former self.

"Ah, fairy essence, how I hungered for it!" Luzee breathed. Blue veins the color of Diana's light popped out of Luzee's pale face, pulsing as it soaked in the fairy's power. She pointed her staff at Remauld. "I will take your essence next."

Ducking under the stone protrusion that hid them from Luzee's view, Jiho pleaded with Koko to try to harness her dragon magic.

"We're running out of time!"

"I don't know what to do!"

"Whatever you do, do it fast," Micah said. "She's killing your friend."

Koko sobbed.

"Don't think, just concentrate," Jiho said. He shot Micah a warning look. They all knew what was at stake.

"Sorry," Micah mouthed back at Jiho.

Leaving Koko, Jiho crawled over to whisper in Micah's ear.

"We need all the help we can get. Is there any chance you can get close enough to free Master Zaki?" Jiho asked. He pointed to where the little namushin master stood off to the side, closer to where they were hidden out on the veranda.

Micah measured the distance between them, Zaki, and Luzee.

"I can try," she said. "But please, make her hurry."

Taking a deep breath, Micah crawled away.

Koko swallowed hard and took a deep breath. "I'm going to try to transform now," she said.

She sat with her back to the veranda wall and closed her eyes, trying to focus on her inner magic. A scream of pain jarred her, and she lost her focus.

"Don't pay attention to anything but your magic," Jiho

urged. "Cover your ears. Listen only to your voice inside."

As Koko breathed in and out, Jiho kept an eye on Micah. He could see when she reached Zaki's side. She was quietly unlocking the manacles on his feet as Luzee was finishing with Diana. When the last blue light was sucked out of the once-powerful fairy, Luzee released her. Diana fell to the ground in a heap of skin and bones, more dead than alive. Luzee then dragged Remauld through the air and into her grasp.

"Now it's your turn, wizard," she breathed.

Remauld fought hard, lashing out at Luzee with his iron manacles and refusing to open his mouth, no matter how punishing the magic she unleashed on him.

Micah was now working on freeing Zaki's hands when suddenly Kai yelled out.

"My lady, my sister is trying to free the prisoners!"

Luzee dropped the exhausted wizard and surged forward to where Kai stood, pointing to his sister. Micah froze, stunned at her brother's betrayal.

"Micah dearest, whatever are you doing?"

The bandit leader ignored her, instead staring in shock at her brother.

"Kai, I'm your sister. How could you betray me?"

"Easy," Kai replied with a sardonic smile. "Besides, it's not the first time."

"What do you mean?"

"I wasn't kidnapped by Roku. I agreed to go along with

his plan because I was sick of the clan. And you."

"Kai . . ." Micah was heartbroken and yet grimly unsurprised.

"You're my little sister, Micah, you're not supposed to be my chief," he snapped. "All because of a stupid gender law."

Kai turned to Luzee. "You can't trust her, but you can trust me. I will serve you loyally."

Luzee brushed him aside, all her attention on Micah.

"Micah, my child, you are confused. Come to my side. Come to me right now and all will be forgiven."

Tearing her eyes away from her traitorous brother, Micah stared into the fairy's cold silver eyes, and suddenly they flashed into Samena's icy-blue ones, before turning back. This fairy was playing with her. Micah's expression hardened. She was angry.

"I don't answer to you!"

One moment she was next to Zaki, and the next she was floating high in the air, gasping for breath.

"Tsk, tsk. Such insolence toward your master," Luzee said.

"You are not my master!" Micah yelled defiantly.

"Oh, but I am," Luzee said as her face morphed smoothly from Samena's to her own. "She is me, and I am your lady, who you swore allegiance to. Yet you dare to betray me. Just like the dragon queen Nanami did before you."

"I'm not Nanami!"

Luzee's face grew dark with anger. "You're just like her!

You were supposed to be my loyal servant. My trusted confidant. You were supposed to be by my side forever. You were supposed to love me."

"I hate you!" Micah shouted.

Scared for Micah, Jiho urged Koko to hurry. "We don't have any more time!"

He could see she was trying—her skin kept shifting and stretching and bubbling.

"Hate me?" Luzee asked with a cruel smile. "You don't know what it feels like to truly loathe someone. But I will show you."

Micah started screaming in pain.

Jiho couldn't take it. He couldn't let her suffer when it was his fault that she was dying. He jumped to his feet. He had to do something. But before he could make a move, something shoved him hard from behind. He turned to see a huge dragon with shimmering golden scales, a thick blue-black mane, and big fierce eyes. It roared so hard it shook the entire castle and growled deep and low in its throat.

"No, it can't be!" Luzee shouted. "I killed all of you."

Koko bellowed and leaped forward to attack Luzee.

"This time I will make sure you stay dead, Nanami!"

Electricity surged between Luzee's hands and formed a white ball of current, which she launched at Koko.

"No!" Jiho grabbed Koko by the leg as the lightning ball hit her in her dragon chest. It lifted her up in the air, away from Jiho, and sent her soaring over the walls.

"Koko!" Jiho stumbled to the wall and looked over. But he could see nothing but the broken treetops where Koko's body had crashed through them.

"And just like that, dragons are once again extinct," Luzee drawled.

Jiho sobbed. His mind filled with images of Koko laughing and crying. His friend was dead. Grief was swept aside as rage filled him. His friend was dead. The last dragon in the world was gone. Evil walked the world again.

Anger that was lava hot threatened to choke him. His chest heaved painfully, and his thoughts were chaotic and violent. He saw Luzee pick up Remauld again. It reminded him of Koko and riding the clouds, her face laughing at him.

She was gone.

Jiho screamed in fury. He pulled out his slingshot and flung a large rock right at Luzee's nose.

"Ow!" Luzee was stunned. Black blood dripped from her nose. "How dare you!"

She threw a lightning bolt at Jiho but it missed him completely, cracking the floor at his right foot. Another rock hit Luzee square in the forehead.

Howling with rage, Luzee shot bolt after bolt at him in rapid-fire order, but they all missed him. One hit Kai as he tried to reach for Jiho's slingshot. Another ricocheted across the room and lit up Brock Murtagh, who was trying to escape.

Jiho shot rock after rock as he methodically closed the gap between him and the evil fairy. Black blood dripped from open wounds on Luzee's face inflicted by his shots. She threw Remauld to the floor.

"Your deflection power is strong," Luzee gritted between her teeth. "I will have it."

She leaped forward and slammed the blood egg on Jiho's forehead. Dazed, Jiho opened his mouth in pain, letting out a purple strand of light. Luzee pounced on it and began to inhale the light.

"Your essence tastes so strange," Luzee said.

Jiho tried to grab the staff to nullify the magic, when he realized something.

"My essence nullifies magic," he whispered to himself.

He looked at Luzee's wild silver eyes as she greedily sucked in his magical essence. Something within him seemed to be collapsing. He felt weak in a way he'd never experienced before. As if she was sucking his bones dry. But he knew he had to let her have his magic, take it into her core. The veins of her face, under the black blood, popped out and turned purple, like Jiho's essence.

Taking his last rock from his pocket, he punched Luzee hard in the eye. Stunned, Luzee dropped Jiho and stumbled back. This time, the blood that coursed from her head was red, not black.

Jiho smiled through his pain and shouted, "Luzee has lost her power, she can be killed now!" Hoping that someone, anyone would hear him.

Hissing in fury, Luzee tried to strike Jiho with a lightning bolt, but could not conjure up any magic.

"What's happening?"

"My essence nullifies magic," Jiho shouted. "It is my greatest power!"

"That can't be! I am the strongest fairy in the world!"

"Used to be," Jiho taunted. "You're not so tough now!"

"You tricked me!" Luzee screamed, then lurched for the long jagged black dagger that lay on the ground before her and stabbed Jiho through the stomach.

Searing pain, blinding and horrifying, overwhelmed Jiho. He fell to his knees. He had failed.

"Who's laughing now?" Luzee shouted fiercely.

Looking at the fairy's nightmare-like face, Jiho wondered why he'd ever thought she was beautiful.

A familiar bellow filled the air, and a golden blur of motion launched itself on Luzee. Jiho fell hard to the ground and saw Koko grasp Luzee by her claws and throw her across the room onto the veranda.

"Koko," he whispered. "You're alive."

Koko slowly stalked the fairy, anger vibrating every scale of her body, so that they let off a metallic thrumming sound that was menacing to hear.

Luzee pointed the staff at Koko. "Stay back, dragon! I command you to stop!"

Koko growled as she closed the distance between them.

"Stop, beast!" Luzee shouted as she shook the staff at Koko. Nothing happened. With a scream of frustration, Luzee threw the staff at Koko's head.

Koko flew up into the sky and nose-dived onto the fairy, piercing her with her sharp talons. Luzee's body jerked and then stilled, her silver eyes still open in shock. As her last breath left her body, purple and blue essences slowly floated away.

Koko lurched over to where Jiho lay gasping in pain.

"Is she dead? Are we all safe?" he asked.

Koko nodded her great dragon's head solemnly.

"Good," Jiho said. He gazed up at Koko with eyes that were starting to dim.

"I thought you were dead." Tears seeped from the corners of his eyes.

Koko turned and roared at the masters, who were now releasing themselves from their manacles with Micah's help. Diana, who had been a desiccated body just minutes before, returned to her natural form upon Luzee's death. They came to Koko's side, gazing sadly at Jiho.

"There is nothing we can do to save him," Aeria said gently.

Koko's dragon roar was pitifully sad as she turned back to her friend.

"It's okay, Koko. I'm so glad I got to see you again."

Koko let out a soft mournful noise that sounded just like her cry in her human form.

"Thank you, Koko," Jiho gasped. "I've always wanted to see a real dragon." And then the light in his eyes went out as they gazed sightlessly at the sky. Koko let out an agonized bellow and nuzzled her head against Jiho's still form. The dragon curled into a ball and laid her head on top of her friend's still chest. One large teardrop rolled down her face and splashed on Jiho's body.

CHAPTER 27

THEN, SUDDENLY, JIHO's eyes blinked and he expelled a shaky breath. The masters shouted in shocked delight.

"Jiho!" Aeria beamed. "You're alive!"

"What happened?" he asked in confusion.

He stared up at Koko's dragon self and the shimmer of tears in her large dragon eyes.

"Dragon's tears," Aeria said. "A dragon can't cry unless they feel true love. A dragon's tears are the most powerful magic in the world."

"But he nullifies magic," Zaki said in confusion.

"He was also dying," Aeria responded gently.

"We have witnessed a miracle today," Remauld said in relief.

"Several miracles," Diana replied. "I think I owe him a great apology."

"I think it can wait for now," Zaki chimed in, as he motioned for all the masters to step back, giving the boy and the dragon some space.

Jiho stood up and looked down at his shirt, where blood stained a gaping hole in his abdomen.

"You saved me!" He smiled up at Koko as her tears continued to drip down onto his face.

"We should bottle this and sell it for a lot of money," he said with a laugh. But then he stilled, slapping a hand to his wet face. "Papa!"

He ran to the back of the room, and knelt by his father's side, next to Koko's parents.

"Don't worry, Jiho," the queen said. "He slept through it all."

The king and queen then rose to their feet and left him, calling Koko's name. Jiho realized they didn't know that she'd turned into a dragon. But he had to focus on his father first.

Jiho pressed his wet hand on his father's chest and waited. After a long tense moment, his father opened his eyes.

"Jiho, my son!" Ranger Park sat up and hugged Jiho hard. Pulling away, Jiho was surprised to find matching tears in his father's eyes.

"How's this possible?"

Jiho smiled. "Today we found out that there are two things that are more powerful than the Parks. The staff of ki and dragon tears."

Ranger Park hugged his son again and rose to his feet. "Well, I can take care of one problem right away."

They walked out to the veranda, where the staff of ki lay broken by Luzee's body. The blood egg had dissolved into a pool of blood and the moonstones had cracked. The masters joined them to stare down at the remains of the greatest evil, vanquished. Diana picked up the staff and removed the moonstones. She handed the now naked staff to Ranger Park.

"Let's make sure this never happens again," she said.

Ranger Park held the staff in his hands and turned to Jiho. "Is this too much of a burden for you, my son?"

Hesitantly Jiho took the staff from his father and examined it. Looking up at his father, he smiled and gave it back. "Guess you'll have to train me more so that I'll be ready for it someday."

His father pulled him into a big bear hug. "That's my boy!"

From the corner of his eye he caught sight of Micah sitting next to her brother's body, holding his hand. He walked over to see that Kai was dead, killed by Luzee's lightning strike.

"I'm sorry, Micah," he said.

Micah shook her head. "Don't be. He was no longer my

brother. He was a traitor to the Botan clan. I just didn't see it until it was too late." She wiped away her tears and stood up. "It's time for me to go home."

Jiho bowed. "Thank you for saving us," he said.

Micah smiled and bowed back. "Actually, you saved me." She gestured to where Koko in her dragon form sat next to the king and queen. "I'm gonna sneak off while everyone is distracted," she said. "Say 'bye to the princess for me."

With a final wave, Micah walked away and quietly disappeared. Jiho thought of how strange it was that the person he distrusted the most turned out to be the one who saved them.

A sudden mournful cry caught his attention. The king and queen sat close by Koko's side, embracing as much of her as they could. Koko looked over to him with her sad dragon's eyes.

The queen beckoned him over. "She can't change back," she said. "Please help her."

Jiho nodded and reached over to hug Koko, but nothing happened.

Pulling away, he was puzzled to find that Koko was still a dragon. "I don't understand why you haven't changed." He hugged her again.

No, Jiho. You can't change me back, because this isn't magic. Koko's thoughts entered his head. *This is who I am.*

"What do you mean, who you are? You're Princess

Koko, future leader of Joson."

I am. But I am also a dragon. It's time I understood what that really means. I am the last dragon in the entire world.

Koko let out a mournful sound and lowered her head.

Jiho put a comforting hand on Koko's neck.

"You'll always be Koko to me," he said.

The boy and the dragon sat together watching the sunset across the vast beauty of the Kidahara.

ACKNOWLEDGMENTS

To my brilliant, dearest editor, Alyson Day. This is our fifth book together and I couldn't be happier or prouder to be working with you! But is it really work when you make it so fun and easy? Okay, not always easy. But always fun and joyous!

And can we talk about the cover? The COVER! I'm pretty sure that Joel Tippie of our Harper art team is an Art Genius! He has always delivered the most amazing and glorious covers for all my books! And Matt Rockefeller, who has now given me three beautiful illustrated covers, delivered exactly the cover I was dreaming of with *The Dragon Egg Princess*. Joel and Matt, you are an author's dream team!

I'm truly blessed and extremely proud of being a Harper-Collins Children's Books author! My Dragon Egg team is simply the best in publishing—Megan Ilnitzki, Manny Blasco, Kathryn Silsand, Laura Mock, Vaishali Nayak, and Jacquelynn Burke—You Guys Rock!

Special thanks to my wonderful agent, Marietta Zacker of Galt & Zacker agency, who absolutely gets me, and that is truly a beautiful thing.

Thanks to Barry Goldblatt, Tricia Ready, and Jennifer Udden at BG Literary Agency for all their support.

And then there are my people. Dhonielle Clayton, Olugbemisola Rhuday-Perkovich, Caroline Richmond, Lamar Giles, Phoebe Yeh, Linda Sue Park, Anne Ursu, Soman Chainani, Sona Charaipotra, Preeti Chibber, Mike Jung, Martha White, Cindy Pon, Elsie Chapman, Justine Larbalestier, Hena Khan, Minh Le, Meg Medina, Will Alexander, Breanna McDaniels, Sarah Park Dahlen, Virginia and John Rah, and Terry Hong. My people who have read for me, cared for me, supported me, fed me, drank with me, cried with me, laughed with me, and have always had my back. I love you all.

To my mom, who always supports me and my books, even though she still asks me if I'm ever going back to practicing law. Sorry, Mom. I'd rather have a root canal.

To my sister, Janet, who always has my back; to my brother-in-law Laurent, who always cooks delicious French food for me; to my niece and nephew, Sebastien and Julia—read this book. I'll give you ten bucks each.

To my awesome, wonderful, love you madly kids,

Summer, Skye, and Graysin. Thank you for reading and brainstorming and helping bring this book to life. Actually, that was just to Summer and Graysin because Skye never reads books. But we keep hoping . . .

Lastly, I want to thank my husband, Sonny, for everything. I'll never forget all those years ago when he turned to me and said, "Quit talking about it and just write the damn book already!" Over fifteen years later, his encouragement and love has gotten me to where I am now and I will forever be grateful that he pushed me into my writing career.

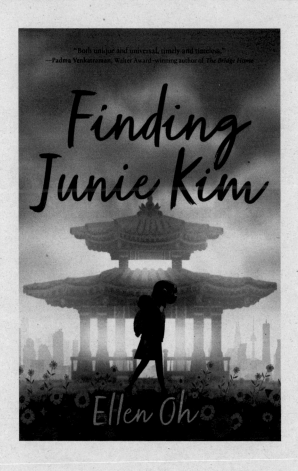

"Both unique and universal, timely and timeless."
—Padma Venkatraman, Walter Award–winning author of *The Bridge Home*

*Finding
Junie Kim*

Ellen Oh

Chapter 1

AUGUST IS STILL THE SUMMERTIME. So why do we have to go back to school? Shouldn't school start in September, when the summer is actually over? I don't get it. It's literally only a week away.

"Junie, hurry up or you'll miss the bus!"

The first day of school and I'm already filled with that horrible empty-stomach crampy feeling of dread.

"Junie!"

I can hear the slight annoyance in my mom's voice and yet I'm still frozen in place in my room, staring at my schoolbag. It's a brand-new messenger bag, dark gray with bright red straps, just like I wanted. But it also means going back to the terrible place.

Middle school.

"Junie Kim!"

"I'm coming!"

Grabbing my bag, I force myself to walk downstairs to the kitchen, where my mom is waiting. On the table is a peanut-butter-and-jelly waffle sandwich and a tall glass of milk. It's what I call my power breakfast, and it's my favorite. But today the thought of eating it makes my throat close up.

"You're gonna have to wolf that down fast, honey."

I shake my head. "I'm not hungry."

"Eat a little anyway," she says, pushing me into my seat. "You need to eat breakfast to get through the day."

She packs my lunch sack into my schoolbag and picks up a big stack of files. My mom is a lawyer with the Department of Justice. It sounds really cool, but it keeps her really busy. That's not as cool.

"Mom, can't you drive me to school today? I don't mind if I'm there early."

She shakes her head regretfully. "I'm sorry, honey, but I have a meeting and I have to run now. Otherwise I'll be late."

There will be no escaping hell this morning.

It's the worst thing in the world that my best friends don't live near me, and therefore I have no one to ride the bus with. It would make the trip bearable. At least last year my older brother was on the bus with me. But now he's going to high school. I'll be all alone with the current worst person of Livingston Middle School.

The walk to the bus stop is only a few blocks from my house, but it reminds me of a nightmare I always have. It

4

starts with a scary chase sequence and ends with me falling off a building, where the fall feels like an intense forever as I scream and scream and then I finally jerk awake. The problem with the falling nightmare is that even after waking up, I'm still scared, as if there's more to come. That's what it feels like reaching the bus stop. I don't know what else is coming, but I know it will be bad.

"Hey, it's the North Korean commie!"

Taking the middle-school bus every morning means listening to Tobias Rodney Thornton, the resident bully, spew racist hate at the only Asian student on the bus. That would be me. Junie Kim. I'm not the only nonwhite kid on the bus. But Tobias doesn't mess with the Black or Latino boys, at least on the bus. Because there are more than one of them.

Tobias is nothing but a bully and a coward, just like his older brother, Satan. Actually, his real name is Samuel Austin Thornton, but Satan suits him better.

Nobody likes either of the Thornton brothers. They're both big and mean and don't care about what other people think of them. And Tobias is five foot ten and probably like two hundred pounds, so he could pummel anyone's opinions into the sidewalk.

As long as I've had to deal with him, I've only ever seen him show two emotions: angry and more angry.

This morning he looks like he's his normal mean.

"Commie!" he spits out as I scurry as far away from him as I can. The bus stop is on the corner of the local park, so there's a lot of space for all of us to spread out. It's one of the biggest stops, with anywhere from fifteen to twenty kids waiting every day. Since Tobias has planted himself on the grassy corner of the park, I rush over to the end of the sidewalk and stand next to a No Parking sign. I pray under my breath that he stays on the park side, but today is not my lucky day.

"Can't you hear me talking to you, dog eater?"

I hunch up like a sad turtle and try to ignore him, but he's now throwing sticks and dirt at me.

I look around, hoping something else will grab his attention.

Megan and her little clique huddle together, as far away from me as possible. We haven't gotten along since I won first place for the sixth-grade essay contest and she got second. She's never forgiven me for doing better in an English class when I was "foreign," and she was American. Truth is, even though I was born and raised here, I'll never be truly American to her.

I'm friendlier with some of the boys, but right now everyone is just trying to avoid Tobias's attention, and since he's focused on me, they're all earnestly avoiding my eyes.

Everyone's too afraid of him to stick up for me. I am overwhelmed with this weird feeling that is sadness, but in a way I've never felt before. It feels like hopelessness. It feels like this is the rest of my life.

The bus pulls up and I rush over to it. Since we're the first stop, it's completely empty. Even though it isn't cool to sit in the front, I make sure to sit near the bus driver. Tobias is mean but not stupid. Our bus driver is not the friendliest man. He is no-nonsense and does not like troublemakers. He keeps the rowdier kids in line by standing up and glaring. Since he looks like he wrestles alligators for fun, it's very effective.

The bus has a hierarchy to it. All the sixth graders have to sit in the front of the bus, while all the eighth graders lord it over everyone else in the back. Seventh graders sit in the middle or as close to the back as the eighth graders will allow. Since Tobias has claimed the back of the bus as his domain, I stay as far away from him as I can. In fact, I'd sit on top of the bus if I could, to avoid breathing the same air as him. While there's only a few stops after ours, it always feels like the longest ride.

Livingston Middle School is a big, boxy red building that looks like a prison. We pull into the school parking lot and immediately notice that there are several police cars in front of the building. Usually there's at least one police car every morning. But four of them? Something must be up.

Inside, everyone is speaking in hushed tones. The teachers don't say good morning. They all look so serious.

The pale-yellow hallways are crowded with students, which is unusual. Sixth graders head straight to the cafeteria and seventh and eighth graders are supposed to line up in the gym before first period. But it looks like no one is in the gym. In the crowd I spot my best friends, Patrice and Amy. I weave over to them and see that Amy is crying and Patrice looks ready to hit something or someone. This is not surprising, because they are usually opposites in almost all ways. Patrice is model beautiful and always wears her thick black hair slicked back and pulled tight into a low ponytail. Her dark brown skin is absolutely flawless. Meanwhile, Amy has bushy, curly blond hair that springs out everywhere and a ghostly-white complexion that shows her multitude of freckles.

"What's wrong?"

"Junie! Someone sprayed swastikas and racist graffiti all over the gym walls!" Patrice says angrily.

My mouth drops open in shock. "Did you see it?"

Patrice shakes her head. "They won't let any of us in since the police are here. But everyone's talking about it. It was targeting Blacks, Jews, and Asians."

"That's literally the three of us!" Amy suddenly looks really scared. "Do you think it was meant for us?"

Patrice bites her lip. "It's not like we're the only ones . . ."

"Does anyone know what it actually said?" I ask.

"I think only the teachers know for sure," Patrice says. "And they're taking it really seriously."

"I don't want to see it," Amy replies. "Just hearing about it is awful. Who would hate us that much?"

We glance down the hallway where we see all the head administrators hovering around the gym doors. The morning bell rings, and the hallway fills with moving bodies. It's loud, but not the normal boisterousness of a middle-school morning.

Patrice and I walk to English together while Amy leaves for her math class. None of us talk; we just wave. I feel lethargic and tired and I'm not even in first period yet. I look over at Patrice, who is walking quietly next to me, her eyebrows furrowed. I can feel the intensity of her emotions radiating from her. I rub her shoulder, and she gives me the saddest smile. In class we sit at our seats and are immediately surrounded by classmates.

"Did you hear what it said?"

"Who could it be?"

"Was it someone from our school?"

I don't know how to respond, so I stay quiet, but I can see Patrice trying to hold back her temper.

Second bell rings, and Ms. Simon tells everyone to take their seats.

Suddenly, the PA system crackles, and we hear the principal's voice over the loudspeaker.

"Good morning. This is Principal Sumner, and I am very sorry to have to start this day, our first day back to school, with such terrible news. Hateful racist and anti-Semitic graffiti was found in our gym. Hate has no place in this school, and we denounce this terrible criminal act. Our school is a place where all must feel free to learn, free of fear and hate. We must remind ourselves that our community stands for welcoming everyone, and it is our responsibility to provide a safe and welcoming environment. There is much work that we need to do, and there is healing that our community will need. An email has been sent to all parents this morning, and counselors will be available to speak with any student who needs their services.

"Due to this criminal act, our beautiful gym has been defaced. Therefore, all gym activities will be held outside today. Rest assured that we are taking this incident very seriously and will investigate this matter thoroughly with the Montgomery County police, and appropriate action will be taken against the perpetrators. We encourage anyone with information to come and talk to staff. This horrible act is not representative of our school and our student body and will not be tolerated."

When he signs off, the classroom erupts in conversation.

Ms. Simon claps her hands several times to get our attention. "I know it's hard to concentrate right now, but we do have a lesson to get through."

Roland Mathers, who is kind of a know-it-all and talks like he's forty, raises his hand and starts to speak even before she calls on him. "Ms. Simon, can you at least tell us exactly what was written on the walls? I think we should know what the vandals said about our community and if any of us might be in danger."

Ms. Simon purses her lips. "I can't tell you the exact nature of what was said, but I can tell you there were no direct threats. Just hateful words specifically aimed at the

Black, Jewish, and Asian communities."

Patrice's hand shoots up in the air. "But Ms. Simon, doesn't the very fact that racist and anti-Semitic words were used make it a threat?"

I tense up at her question. This is our first day with Ms. Simon, who is a middle-aged white lady, and I worry that she might be the type who doesn't get it.

Ms. Simon nods. "You're absolutely right, and I apologize. While no specific threats of harm were written, the very nature of the words themselves was meant to cause fear and intimidation. It is in fact a hate crime, which is why the police are involved. I know it's frightening, but I assure you that the administration and the police are going to make sure that these perpetrators, whoever they are, are caught and punished."

I can see Patrice is as relieved as I am to hear Ms. Simon speak so forcefully and call it a hate crime. She seems like a good teacher, one who really cares.

It's hard to focus on classes after that. I keep wondering what exactly was written on the walls. How bad was it? In the hallways, nobody can talk about anything else, and rumors are all over the place. I hear bits and pieces as I walk by groups of students. Some are clearly shocked and afraid, while others are excited by the most interesting thing to happen in Livingston in a long time.

"I heard there were KKK symbols and that it said to deport all immigrants."

"They said the handwriting looked like it had to be a student."

"Well, it can't be someone who goes here because they broke in late at night, and who would want to come back to school if they didn't have to?"

"I don't believe it. It's all fake news. . . ."

Ugh, I really hate the term *fake news*. I whip my head around to see who made the last comment and am not surprised to see it's one of the obnoxious boys wearing a red *Make America Great Again* hat. It was my mom who explained to me that the slogan was about exclusion and not inclusion. Who they didn't want in this country, in order to make it a world they wanted. It's why it hurts so much to see those hats. It makes me feel unwelcome in my own birthplace, and the country of my parents. The hats remind me of all the people who will never accept me as a real American.

Patrice grabs my hand, and I turn to see the anger tightening her lips into a straight line.

The boy knows we've heard him, and he starts following us and chanting "Fake news! Fake news!" and his friends laugh like hyenas. I'm clenching my teeth so hard I can feel my jaw hurt.

Patrice spins around and looks the boy dead in the eye.

"Piss off," she says without raising her voice, but her eyes shoot lasers. The boy raises his hands in surrender, smirks, and turns away.

I wish I was more like Patrice. She's not afraid to confront people, and she never looks foolish doing so.

"I hate the fake newsers," Patrice says. "They do it deliberately. By denying it, they can pretend it doesn't exist. No racism. No global warming. No refugees dying. It's all about denying the truth."

I look at Patrice in awe. Sometimes she sounds so much older than she really is.

She catches me looking and gives me a small smile. "I'm repeating what my parents say."

"I know," I reply. "But it still sounds right when you say it."

Our cafeteria is on the second floor and always feels way overcrowded and noisy. It has an unusual L shape, making it hard to navigate due to the crush of students. We head for our usual table in the far right corner, but have to pass the annoying popular kids' table. They're mostly white except for Esther Song, the only other Korean girl at our school, who never acknowledges my existence. She's one of those Asians who ignores all other Asians because they remind them that they aren't actually white. My mom says it's internalized racism: when racism messes with you so much you hate who you are and wish you were white.

"Hey, Patrice, I bet you did all that vandalism just so you could say racism is still real. Help! I'm Black and a girl and I'm being oppressed!"

Stu Papadopolis is a smirky, two-faced weasel. But he's also popular because he's rich, and some girls think he's good-looking, which I personally don't get. He reminds me of a beady-eyed rat. And he wears so much cologne I literally gag whenever I'm near him. I want to arrest him for air pollution.

Patrice is glaring at him so hard her nostrils are flaring. "Stu, you are such a racist."

He rolls his eyes dramatically, sending his idiot goons into hysterics. "See what I mean? She's always screaming racism! News flash, Patrice, not everything is about race."

"Only a privileged white guy would say that," Patrice snaps at him.

"Now that's racist and sexist!" Stu howls loudly. "I'm gonna report you to the administration. Oh, wait a minute. Nobody cares about white males anymore. Because we have 'privilege.'" He uses finger quotes. "Right. We're the ones that are really being discriminated against."

Patrice is shaking with rage, and I'm so angry I just want to rip Stu's head bald.

"You're a horrible, nasty troll," I shout at him.

"Shut up, Kim Jong Un. Why don't you go back to your own Communist country?"

"This is my country! I was born here!" I'm so angry I can't help but stumble over my words.

"Says who?"

"Says my birth certificate!"

"Pffft, fake news! You can get fake birth certificates from China."

Before I can say another word, Patrice is pulling me away.

"Come on, Junie, don't talk to him. You'll just get frustrated by his stupidness."

I glare at Esther as I leave, but she avoids my eyes even as she laughs with the others. What a traitor. I can't believe she doesn't see how racist all her friends are. Or maybe she does and just doesn't care. None of them do. I see it in the faces of kids who are rolling their eyes and laughing about the vandalism. What Patrice and I find so horrifying is just a big joke to them.

Patrice and I cling to each other as we speed over to our table. There's not a lot of students of color at Livingston Middle School, but it's true that we tend to stick together. Patrice says we need to be our own support group because of how openly racist a lot of kids have been ever since the presidential election.

As we sit down next to Amy, I'm reminded again how she is the only white girl at our table.

"Stu Papadopolis is such a jerk!" Patrice says as she plops down on the bench.

"Him and his goon squad are jerks," Hena replies. "Every time they walk by me, they whisper 'terrorist.' I hate them." Hena is Pakistani American, with the most gorgeous set of long black curls that I've ever seen on a human.

Lila and Marisol nod fiercely. "Ugh, they think they're so hilarious. Like calling us burrito and taco and telling us to go back to Mexico," Lila says. "They're so brainless they think that South America means Mexico." Lila is Peruvian

American and Marisol is Cuban American, and they are literally the best of friends. They do everything together and are as close as sisters and as opposite as sugar is to salt. Lila is short and brown, a bubbly fast-talker who always has a bright smile for everyone. Marisol is blond and fair and moody. But somehow their differences don't matter when they can unite in their shared hatred of Stu Papadopolis and his gang of evil trolls.

"And they're getting worse. They love standing in front of doors to block us and calling themselves the wall," Marisol chimes in. "And if we get mad, they tell us to chill out and take a joke. It's not funny."

"Ugh, they're horrible," Patrice says.

Then Lila and Marisol call them a bad word in Spanish that sends everyone into giggles. Even I can't help but smile.